THE BOOK OF BELIAH

CRYTON DAEHRAJ

iUniverse®

THE BOOK OF BELIAH

Author Credits: Author of The Planet of the Elohim

iUniverse books may be ordered through booksellers or by contacting:

iUniverse
1663 Liberty Drive
Bloomington, IN 47403
www.iuniverse.com
844-349-9409

Because of the dynamic nature of the Internet, any web addresses or links contained in this book may have changed since publication and may no longer be valid. The views expressed in this work are solely those of the author and do not necessarily reflect the views of the publisher, and the publisher hereby disclaims any responsibility for them.

Any people depicted in stock imagery provided by Getty Images are models, and such images are being used for illustrative purposes only. Certain stock imagery © Getty Images.

ISBN: 978-1-6632-3782-8 (sc)
ISBN: 978-1-6632-3783-5 (hc)
ISBN: 978-1-6632-3781-1 (e)

Library of Congress Control Number: 2022905847

Print information available on the last page.

iUniverse rev. date: 04/13/2022

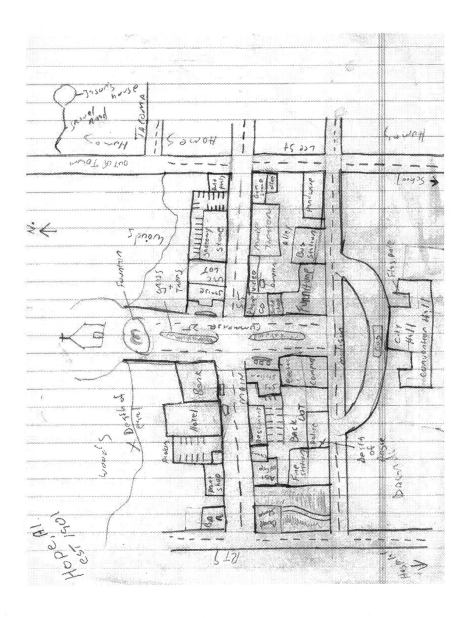

CHAPTER 1

Reality is in the eye of the beholder
From The Book of Beliah
Verse 13

1

JASON BECAME CONSCIOUS OF HIMSELF in the dreamy landscape of another world, another dimension. He knew he had been here before, but never at this level of consciousness. He took note of his surroundings and found it to be a gently rolling, pale-white terrain with the apparent texture of melted marshmallow.

Trying to retrace his last disconnected memory, thoughts of why he was here and how raced through his mind, disturbing him with feelings of death. Suddenly, a small glob of his environment, bluish in color and the size of a basketball solidified before his eyes and started floating towards him, seemingly suspended in mid air. It stopped moving a few feet short of him and hovered approximately four feet off of the ground. Without warning the bright, spherical glob contracted in size, turned dark blue and then expanded, like a spaceship coming out of hyperspace, rapidly filling the environment surrounding Jason.

The expanding, blue orb engulfed his awareness within moments and he found himself tumbling into a panorama of words and sounds. The words he encountered within this sphere formed a symphony of pictures in his mind, each word a form, asking the question, "Why are you here?"

Jason tried to speak, but he couldn't see the words he was trying to say. Nothing came out. The pictorial expressions, although moving and flowing, swimming naturally in this environment, withdrew from him, disappearing through an open window in space. Once the word/picture forms had passed through, the window, timeless and pre-existing, remained opened and he started for it, his body floating like an un-tethered balloon, guided by his thoughts alone.

Through the window, following the words, he entered a rushing current of air, blasting him out of control. As his consciousness stretched thin like a piece of spaghetti, his thoughts latched on to one of the words, hoping it would carry him to the birthplace of those graphic melodies.

His mode of travel terminated and the question he was pursuing melted into an intensely glowing, ethereal Being. Although it lacked any real form, this entity had a shape and a sex: it was definitely feminine! She had that same bluish tint as those words and looked like an upside down egg with half a dozen long, slender, wispy tentacles. There was one tentacle coming out of its top and one coming from the bottom; the remaining four came out and around her midsection.

Jason was overwhelmed by her attractive allure, but couldn't decide if she was beautiful by earthly standards. It was her alien-ness that made it difficult and so he let his first impression stand. He couldn't see through or beyond her for all there was, was her. He felt like a baby seeing his mother for the first time.

She spoke again and her words took form, becoming a life unto itself. The words encompassed him, pulsating with visual energy and once again he lost himself within her words. He felt what she felt as she spoke. "You must not be here. Go back and find yourself, return to your body. There will be time enough for this later."

Although he longed to remain with her, he wanted to return to his own space and time. "Yes, later," he said, his words taking the form of clouds out of his mouth and joined with her in what Jason could only describe as intimacy. The moment after their union, the glowing orb, with her inside, rapidly collapsed into nothing. The effect was quite dramatic and left Jason dazed. *She's gone,* he thought, and instantly was transported back to his bedroom where he awoke lying on his back in a pool of sweat, staring up at the ceiling.

2

If it weren't for that now familiar buzzing sensation, Jason wouldn't have known he had been asleep. His whole body tingled. The sweat dripping from his hairline gathered in his ears and a strong odor filled his nostrils. The sensation made him think of running, but running had nothing to do with the sweat or the tingling. What had happened to him definitely wasn't physical. He knew the sweat was from the memory of the experience rather than from anything he did while in that state.

He blinked several times trying to clear his head of the vision but to no avail. He feared if he screamed out, as his mind demanded him to, reality would flood in on him and banish the experience to the depths of his subconscious. That, he reminded himself, he wouldn't do. The times before he had given in to that impulse, he found that sanctuary in the physical realm only haunted his dream realm. He would have to ride out the experience.

The rays of dawn filtered in through the crack between the curtains and struck Jason harshly in the face. He turned his eyes away from the glare and got out of bed, still groggy, needing to go to the bathroom. Tonka, his dog, lying on the floor next to his bed, rolled to his side in response, expecting his belly to be rubbed. Jason obliged with the ball of his foot. "Good boy," he croaked.

The wooden floor felt cool to his feet as he stumbled towards the bathroom. He turned on the faucet and grabbed a washcloth to mop the sweat off of his face. Looking into the mirror he said, "I've got to tell someone about these dreams." His blue eyes were bloodshot from the broken sleep of the past couple of nights. The dreams had become a nightly affair.

"The last time I told Tommy about them," he said, turning away from the mirror. "He said I was watching too much of the X-Files."

Tonka cocked his head to one side as if trying to understand his master. He's a smart dog, Jason thought.

"If it's a dream," he continued, "then why does it feel so real? What do you think, boy?"

Tonka lowered his head between his paws and closed his eyes. He didn't have a clue as to what Jason was asking.

"How can I explain the unexplainable?" He sat down on the bed and glanced at the clock. It read: 5:12 a.m. "Here it is my day off and I'm wide awake at five in the morning. There ain't no justice."

Visions of what had happened troubled him. The sights he had witnessed over the last few nights were too incredible to believe. How could he tell anyone about them if he wasn't sure of the reality of those visions? He use to think of the experiences as dreams, but now they were getting too real. Tumbling face down on his bed, Jason fell into a groggy, semi-conscious sleep. Two hours later, forcing his self awake, Jason got up, dressed and went downstairs.

He decided to skip breakfast and headed over to Tommy's house, located just behind his at the end of a dirt path through a small section of trees.

Jason knocked on the back door and said, "Tommy, you up?"

Tommy pulled the curtain aside and said, "Hey, Jason. We still on for the movie today?"

"Yeah, but I want to go to Lazenby's first. I want to check somethin' out."

"Okay. Are you hungry?"

"Nah. I didn't sleep too good last night."

They started down Tacoma road and Tommy said, "You look like crap."

"Thanks jerk," Jason said. Then, quietly, "I... I've been having those dreams again."

"The ones about you leaving your body and stuff?"

"Yeah. I want to see if Lazenby's has any books on it. I can't tell you how real they feel. It's like I'm in another world or something. And—" He started to tell Tommy about the female... Thing! But then decided against it.

"And what?"

"And I think they might be real is all."

"I think you're neurotic."

"You're an asshole. Betcha popcorn I beat you there."

"You're on."

The two high-school graduates raced down Tacoma and crossed Lee Street ending up behind the grocery store. Jason cut through a vacant lot and darted west down Main Street; Tommy was close on his heels. They passed through the intersection of Commerce Street and Jason kicked it into high gear. Lazenby's bookstore was at the end of Main about a block away and the two boys sprinted the remaining distance. Jason was the clear winner but only by a foot.

"Hey," Jason panted. "You—you let me win."

"Nah. You won. It must be my old age."

"Yeah right. Or maybe Missy wore you out." They laughed at that, and after catching their breath went into the bookstore.

"Hey Tommy. Jason. You boys stayin' out of trouble?" asked a middle-aged, slightly balding, gray-haired man.

"Yes sir, Mr. Lazenby," they said.

"Good and let's keep it that way, right Tommy?"

"Y-Y-Yes sir."

Jason gave Tommy a smirk and elbowed him lightly in the ribs. They wandered to the back of the store and Jason asked, "Is he okay with you and Missy?"

"Yeah, he thinks I might be good for her. Hey, is this what you are looking for?" Tommy pointed to a group of books under a section labeled: "Occult".

"That's it!" Jason reached up and pulled one from the shelf. It was titled: Out-of-Body Experiences, by Robert Monroe. He flipped it open and read some of the Chapter titles.

"You gonna get it?" Tommy asked.

"Maybe. I guess I should get another one by a different author."

"You gonna have money for the movie?"

"Sure. I don't have to buy popcorn, remember."

They made their way to the front of the store and Jason stacked two books on the counter. "What's that?" he asked, pointing to a black and white glossy picture propped up on the counter.

"I don't know," Tommy said. "Some writer's comin' this weekend."

"Here to the bookstore?"

"Sure is," Lazenby said, ringing up the books. "His name is Beliah and he's on tour with his book. That'll be six thirty-seven."

Jason paid him and then asked, "What kind of book?"

"That one there," Lazenby said. "I haven't read it, but it's got something to do with Witches—should be right up your alley. Here."

Jason took the change and walked over to a small bookrack by the door. The book filling up the black, metal rack showed the author's face. There was something disturbing about the face, but he couldn't figure out what. "Is he gonna sign'em?"

"Sure is," said Lazenby. "He's reserved the meetin' hall for Friday night. Gonna have some sort of introduction and then Saturday he'll be here to put his "X" on a couple of books. I might need some help settin' up. Can I count on you, Tommy?"

"Is Missy gonna be here?"

"Would it make a difference?"

"Well..."

"She'll be here. What d'ya say?"

"Okay. Eight o'clock?"

"I'll see you then."

The two boys left the bookstore and crossed over to the north side of Main. They stopped at Sandy's Bar and looked through the plate glass window.

"What you lookin' at?" Tommy asked.

"Nothing," Jason said, and then backed away from the window.

"Boy, I think you're in love with that woman."

"I'm not," Jason said, his cheeks turning a bright red. "Besides, I wasn't looking for her anyway. They don't open until five."

"Uh-huh. C'mon. The movie doesn't start until noon. Let's go to the video store."

"Okay. Hey, do you want to go to that meetin' tomorrow night?"

"You gonna buy his book?"

"Yeah, I was thinking about it."

Tommy lowered his head and shook it while laughing. "You're one weird guy, Jason."

3

The day passed quickly and Jason had a great time with Tommy, but by the end of the day he was ready to go home. It had been fun, but he really wanted to read a couple chapters out of the books he bought before going to sleep. After changing into cut off sweat pants and a ragged-looking Beatles T-shirt, he climbed into bed and took one of the books out of the cream-colored, plastic sack he got at Lazenby's. He was tired and the cool night air stealing its way into the room through a slightly opened window made him drowsy; and after only six pages into the first chapter, he drifted asleep.

As he slept, he became lucid and was very much aware that he was dreaming. The dream was centered within his bedroom and he felt a large, dark presence watching him. He was still dreaming when he heard a voice so cold that it made him deathly afraid.

"Jason," it hissed.

In that one word he heard all the lost souls of Hell cry out. The pain that spewed from this disembodied voice was twisted into one of extreme pleasure. This dark presence thrived on the fear of others and drew strength from that fear, feeding off of the energy generated by fear.

It spoke again saying, "I have come for you."

Jason was possessed by the words like a snake in the charms of a charmer. He was losing himself to the Dark Thing, and when it spoke he lost all will to move. This thing spilled out of nowhere, seeping into Jason's bedroom through a thin slit in space. As it grew, it blanketed his room with a thick, black fog, and a stench of rotting corpses filled his nostrils.

He tried to call out, but only a whisper escaped his lips. *What is this,* he asked mentally. *If this is a dream, why can't I wake up? And if I am awake, how can this creature from Hell really exist?*

It suddenly occurred to him that he must be Out-of-Body, and with that realization he opened his eyes and found his body lying fast asleep below him. He had the sensation of floating just inches away from the ceiling. He studied his prone figure resting comfortable below him, oblivious to the thing sharing the room with him.

"Jason!"

He turned to the voice and saw the thing emit an intense beam of pulsating energy. The beam entered his body and within moments shattered the only body he knew into a thousand pieces. He stared in horror at the destruction, each piece calling out his name as bloody chunks of flesh and bone splattered all over the room. He felt like he was everywhere and nowhere. He knew all and could remember nothing. He realized he didn't exist and yet did in some way separate from his body.

What had happened was beyond his present comprehension and he had neither the faculties nor the desire to contemplate life and death. He felt as though he was part of a greater whole, indistinguishable from anything else. He saw everything and yet knew nothing. He was at peace until...

He woke up. Sluggishly, he felt his face and chest. He was still there. *Was that a dream?* He fell back to sleep with one hand on his face and the other on his chest. *Was that a dream?*

CHAPTER 2

*Science would have us believe that they hold the truth, even
though most of us can't understand it. Shouldn't the truth
be something even the simple can understand?*
From The Book of Beliah
Verse 1

4

BELIAH RODE INTO TOWN DRIVING a jet black Jeep CJ7. The bellow
of the motor was made louder by the custom glass packs running along
the side of the Jeep and extending out by the rear tires. Dust settled on the
windshield as he came to a screeching halt at an intersection. A signpost
directed him down Route Nine to his destination a few miles away. The
sign read: Hope, Alabama. Pop. 1128—5 miles. Beliah smiled to himself
and said, "They won't have any hope after I get through with them."

He gunned the motor then reached up to adjust his rearview mirror.
His piercing, icy-blue eyes had a mark of evil all their own: they resembled
those of a wolf, glassy and hard to read. He threw his head back and laughed
out loud. "Another town will soon be mine."

He shifted the gearbox to first and the transfer to low. He popped
the clutch and a cloud of smoke and macadam erupted from the front
and rear wheels. As he drove toward Hope, shifting the Jeep into higher

gears, the deafening percussion of the exhaust echoed down the tree-lined roadway, and above the hellish noise could be heard the howling laughter of a mad man.

Beliah skidded sideways as he threw the Jeep into first down from forth. To a less experienced driver the Jeep would have toppled over, but the tires held fast, leaving twin streaks of rubber. He sat at the intersection of Route Nine and Main Street with the motor still spitting out "Blam, blam, bla, bla, bla." On his immediate left was a bar, and across Main also to his left was a bookstore: Lazenby's Books!

He eased up on the clutch and motored casually into the parking lot of the bookstore. It was around ten in the morning on a Friday and traffic was light, not only on Main but also in the bookstore itself. Beliah cut off the motor and stepped out on the pavement. In comparison with the height of the jeep, his six feet, two-inch tall build made him appear even larger. The ride in the opened-top vehicle had made his shoulder-length dirty blonde hair lay every which way. Reaching up with one hand, he brushed the hair out of his eyes and back across his head. A ring of sweat was visible under the arms of his denim-blue, button-down shirt.

He placed his hands in his back pockets and stared at the lettering on the front door. He put one black, silver-tipped, booted foot on the curb and read aloud what was written. "Book signing tomorrow. Witchcraft: A Study into the Myth, by Beliah". No last name was given. Below that was a picture of a very handsome man in an open-collared, knit shirt. It was a picture of him. Beliah smiled to himself, the corners of his month twisting up into a hideous sneer. The door of the bookstore opened a crack and the smiling face of a cute high-school girl looked out.

"Hey, ain't you the guy signin' books tomorrow? You're even better lookin' than your picture," she giggled, and then said, "You gonna come in or what?"

"Sure am, sweetheart. Say, do you have a boyfriend?"

"Idda know," she said, blushing deeply.

"Well, if you ever figure out if you do or not, let me know. I'd hate to take you away from some big jock."

"Tommy's not that big."

"Ah, so the truth comes out."

"I mean the thing is he really isn't my boyfriend." That was a lie. She was in love with Tommy.

"What's your name, sweetheart?"

"Missy," she said blushing again. Recovering, she opened the door all the way and stood sideways, giving Beliah a profile of her body. She had large firm young breast that seemed to defy gravity. Her body was well proportioned with a rear that perfectly balanced out her front. Her long, dark-brown hair fell loosely about her face and shoulders.

Missy usually loved to have boys look at her. She had even seen the grown men staring. She was what was known around school as a "Hot mess". She was also known to be a tease. Missy, however, was still a virgin and she used that to her advantage. She would play with the boys and get them all worked up, but at the last minute she would turn innocent and say she couldn't. It was because of her looks that she could get away with it. But this guy was different. This guy made her nervous, but for some reason she knew that she wanted him in the worst of ways. *He could do anything he wants with me,* she thought.

Beliah walked the short distance to the door and stopped. With her holding the door opened, he couldn't get through unless he turned sideways also. She didn't move so he turned to face her and sidestepped through. As he did, Beliah's hand softly brushed against the zipper of her blue jeans. "Are you ever going to let Tommy tag that?"

Her shock at having a grown man touch her there quickly turned to lust. "Maybe I'm saving that for someone else." She was breathing heavily now and her breasts were straining against her white Tee-shirt, slightly moving up and down in time with her breathing.

"So I see," he said.

She blushed for the third time and lowered her eyes out of embarrassment. She took the opportunity to casually glance below his waist. A spot had been slightly worn to one side of his zipper and the fabric of his tight fitting black jeans was even now on the verge of pulling apart. Her eyes widened and a small gasp escaped her lips.

Beliah continued by and entered the store.

The man behind the counter was obviously the owner. His nametag read: Carl Lazenby, owner. Beliah wondered why in a town this small anyone needed a nametag.

"Daddy?" It was Missy. "This is the guy on the book." She held up a copy back side out.

"Yes honey, I see that." Carl was roughly the age Beliah appeared: Thirty-five. He was slightly balding and his remaining hair had turned an ugly color of gray. His swollen belly rested on top of the counter and his arms were stretched out in front supporting his weight.

"Daddy..." Missy ran up to the end of the counter.

"Now go on, honey. Mr. ah... Beliah and I have some business to discuss." Carl said with love in his eyes.

"Okay daddy." Missy skipped away from them and went behind a bookshelf. She moved some books around and opened up a space between the books so she could get a better look at Beliah unseen.

"She sure is a cutie," Beliah said.

"That she is. Not a lick of trouble. Goes to church every Sunday." Carl looked at Beliah and gave him a wide, toothy grin. There were bits of tobacco between his yellowing teeth, stained from years of dipping.

Beliah returned the smile. Oddly enough, Beliah's teeth appeared to have the same discoloring, even though he'd never tried the stuff. *I wonder what you would think about your daughter,* Beliah thought, *if you saw her on her hands and knees barking like a dog and loving it. She's nothing but a whore like the rest of them.* Beliah's smile grew wider.

Carl liked him immediately. He hadn't read Beliah's book, but if this was the man who wrote it then it couldn't be all bad. He reached out his right hand and said, "Hi. The name's Lazenby."

"Beliah and you must be the owner." Beliah shook his hand, pointed to the nametag.

"Yeah, that's me. Usually I don't wear one, but with all of the excitement your book has stirred up, I figured some folks from out of town might be in this weekend."

"So you have everything ready, then?" Beliah said looking around the modest store.

"Sure do. You'll be sittin' right over there," he said, indicating a square, foldout table in the front section of the store. "I've still got most of your books boxed up. I'll have them brought out as you need 'em."

"Good deal, man. Look, I've got a couple of other places I need to check with. Can you tell me how to get to the hotel and the Court House?"

"Sure can. The hotel is just down the street on the left," Carl said, pointing east down Main. "But they won't let you check in until noon. City Hall is at the end of Commerce. Madison runs right in front of it. Best way from here is to take a right at the four-way."

Beliah thanked Carl and walked towards the door. He reached for the knob and abruptly stopped, rotating his head to look over his shoulder.

When he did, he caught Missy peeking at him from between the books. He smiled at her hungrily. She jumped back startled, but then managed to regain her composure long enough to give her own seductive smile.

"You say," Beliah called out to Carl, "that the hotel is just down the street?" He continued looking at Missy to see if she was listening. She was.

"Yeah, but not before noon. That's about a little over an hour from now."

"Thanks." Beliah left the store and looked down the street. He could see the hotel and the intersection Lazenby mentioned. It was about a block away and he decided City Hall couldn't be much further. He started walking. It was a very small town. *The best way to see a town is to walk through it,* he mused.

He crossed the parking lot and went through a gap between two buildings: the Post Office, which faced Main, and the Sheriff Station, which faced Madison. The gap opened into a sizeable back lot that served as employee parking for the various businesses on that block.

The area funneled out onto Madison and he passed between the Electric Company and the Sheriff Station. A hundred yards or so in front and to the left was City Hall. It was a long, rectangular building with more windows than it had rooms. The architecture was quite modest and built of solid, white-washed stones. It sat off of Madison and had a short, half-moon shaped driveway that started from a point on Madison and ended several yards down the road.

He approached the building and climbed the short flight of steps. Moving through the glass door Beliah stopped at a directory and read the few names presented. He noticed that most of the offices were held by the same person and laughed out loud.

"Can I help you?" a voice said from behind him.

"Yes," he said turning to greet the voice. "You can. I'm looking for the auditorium. I will be speaking there tonight."

"Oh, my lands! You're that Belamy fellow—that writer." The voice belonged to a heavy set, middle-aged black woman.

"Actually, the name's Beliah and yes, I'm that writer."

"I should've recognized the face. It's not everyday we gets us a famous writer here." The woman was beaming. "We have it all set up. Damn near the whole town's coming. 'Cuse my language. Come on down this way." She grabbed Beliah tightly by the arm and forcefully dragged him along with her.

A couple of doors down, she stopped. "It's in here," she said opening a set of double doors.

The doors opened into a fairly large room. There were chairs ten deep on both sides of a central aisle. The rows of chairs extended down a gradual slope and ended at a raised platform. Beliah made a quick count of the chairs and found that it could hold about four hundred people.

"This will be perfect," he said. "I'll be here promptly at six o'clock. Should I come directly to you?"

"Oh, my lands! I'm only the custodian. I'm not too sure who would handle this."

"You do have the keys, don't you? Why should I bother anyone else?" Beliah had no desire to talk with anyone else and was tiring of this woman as well. She was too bubbly for his taste. He could sense an amazing goodness about her. That bothered him. He couldn't work his magic on someone this pure.

"You really need to go see the Mayor. I can't..."

"Look," he said harshly, "I have other, more important things to do. Can't you tell the person in charge I'm in town and I will be here at six?"

"I guess I can." Her excited expression changed to one of caution.

"Good. I'll return then." With that, Beliah turned and left.

Outside, the sun was directly overhead and Beliah determined it was just after twelve. He walked down the steps and across the grass to Madison. Commerce was directly in front of him and he started down the center of it on the grassy median. Traffic had picked up since this morning and he accredited that to the lunch hour.

On his right, Beliah passed a soda shop with pictures of ice cream painted on the front window. *That's where the kiddies hang out,* he thought. He made a mental note to stop in there later when school let out.

He stopped at the intersection. The traffic on both sides of Commerce was moving at a steady pace. He looked up at the signal lights and saw them swaying in the slight breeze. He pointed a finger at the lights and they changed to red in all directions. He stepped into the intersection and was almost across when a few cautious drivers eased into the middle. He snickered at the confusion and pointed over his shoulder in the direction of the lights. They went back to normal and horns sounded in every direction.

Beliah entered the hotel and walked up to the front desk. The young man sitting down behind the desk looked up from reading a Men's magazine and recognized him immediately.

"You're that writer." The boy was fresh out of high-school and had a face full of greasy pimples to prove it. He squeezed on one of them as he spoke. "I've seen your picture. I've got your room all ready for ya."

"Great, man. If I can have the key I've got some cleaning up to do."

"I'm coming to the meeting tonight," the boy said, still squeezing zits.

"Is that a fact? Glad to hear it." Beliah eyed the boy and knew he was a virgin. This boy was the kind that sat around on a Friday night playing with himself, and after he was done squeezed zits in the mirror. Pathetic—him I can use him. "The key?"

"Oh, sure… here you go," the boy said nervously as he handed Beliah the key.

Beliah reached for the key and as their fingers lightly touched a small spark jumped from Beliah to the boy. Instantly, the boy's eyes glazed over and he stood deathly straight. If a coroner had seen the sight, he would have thought the boy had died on his feet and rigor mortis had set in. "Come to me later," Beliah said.

"Yesss…"

Beliah took the key and said, "102?"

The boy snapped awake, unsure of his surroundings. "Uh… yeah. Sure."

Beliah walked towards the first room on the right and paused briefly at the room on the left. He felt something from that room, but couldn't make out what. He decided it was nothing and retired to his room.

5

Beliah stepped out of his room at exactly three o'clock. As he passed the front desk, he gave a quick glance in that direction and noticed an older gentleman leaning back in a chair watching TV. He continued out of the hotel heading in the direction of the soda shop. After walking a few minutes, he entered the soda shop and found it filled with kids.

"That's him," a girl said, giggling.

Beliah looked in the direction of the comment and found the voice belonged to Missy. "Hey sweetheart," he said. "Daddy give you time off for good behavior?"

Missy blushed and then said, "I'm daddy's little girl. I can do whatever I want. Wanna sit down?"

Beliah strolled over to a table filled with Missy and two of her girlfriends. Her friends giggled, whispering between themselves and then stood up.

"You don't have to leave on my account," Beliah said.

"Yes we do," one of the girls said. Then both of them looked at Missy and giggled some more.

"See you later, girl," the other one said to Missy. The two teenagers left the soda shop still giggling.

"They're so immature," Missy said.

"It seems to me, sweetheart, that you wanted them to leave." Beliah smiled at her and winked.

She held back a blush and said, "Maybe I did."

"So tell me. Why weren't you in school this morning?"

"Why do you think I should've been in school? How old do you think I am?"

"Judging by your gorgeous body, I'd say at least twenty-one."

The comment caught her off guard and this time she couldn't hide the blush.

"But you aren't, are you?" Beliah locked eyes with her. He could sense the nervous, delicious tension coming off of her.

"No, I'm only seventeen. But I'll be eighteen in June. I got out early to help daddy for tomorrow. I guess you think of me as a little, immature, high-school brat."

Their table got most of the attention from the other kids in the place and Beliah could tell Missy was eating it up. He reached across the table and lightly touched her hand with one well-manicured finger. She gasped but didn't move.

"Who says I have anything against high-schoolers. I find them to be most... refreshing."

Missy's palms grew sweaty and her breathing quickened. She wasn't use to being the one seduced. "W-W-What do you mean by that?" she stuttered.

"Well, sweetheart, let's just say I expected you to show up at the hotel this afternoon. When you didn't show, I came looking for you."

Missy shifted her eyes back and forth to see if anyone heard what was just said. They had been speaking low and the jukebox was playing in the back ground, so she decided they weren't being overheard. Her appearance took on that of a little girl, innocent and sweet. She had always used this look to get anything she wanted. It worked on her father and it worked on Tommy. She lowered her eyes in a shy sort of way and then looked at him out of the corner of her eyes. Her look was no longer sweet. It was one of lust and desire.

"Why were you looking for me?" she said innocently.

"Maybe I like virgins." Beliah found it easy to seduce her. He didn't have to play with her mind any because she already wanted him, bad. "Let's get out of here, sweetheart."

"But I can't. I mean, what if someone sees us?"

"You can just tell them I had some questions about the book signing tomorrow. Tell them you volunteered to drive me over to your father's place. You did drive here, didn't you?"

"Yeah, I did, but you can't touch me until after we leave. I'm parked at the furniture store next door."

"Lead the way."

They stood up and walked out the door. Reaching the parking lot, she quickly unlocked the door of a white 300ZX Turbo and slid behind the wheel. Beliah climbed in the other side and she peeled out of the space leaving twin rubber tracks.

The reality of what she was doing and about to do dawned on her. She was a virgin and was about to lose her virginity to a man old enough to be her father. The idea excited and scared her. She floored the car through the intersection and rounded the corner onto Main. She felt a hunger in the pit of her stomach. She wasn't hungry—this was more of a burning. She swung the car into the restaurant parking lot and drove around back. "I can't let anyone see my car at the hotel," she said.

They got out of the car and Missy bolted across the street. She had to run with one arm over her breast to keep them from bouncing; she hardly ever wore a bra. She reached the other side and stood under the awing of the hotel. She was scared to death. *Oh God,* she thought. *I'll die if someone sees me.*

Missy opened the first set of glass doors and stopped dead. She drew herself up against the wall in between the inner and outer doors, looking like she had seen a ghost.

"What's the matter, sweetheart?" Beliah asked, coming up behind her.

"The old guy, the one behind the desk, I know him. He's a friend of my father's. If I go in there he's bound to tell him."

"Don't worry about him. He won't see a thing. I promise."

"You don't understand. If he sees me...! Look, I really shouldn't be here. I'm not..."

"I said don't worry. Trust me, sweetheart."

Beliah stared into her eyes and she melted. Some part of her mind told her to just turn around and leave. This has been fun, but enough was enough. She tried, but quickly realized she didn't have a choice, not any more.

Beliah grabbed her arm and hauled her through the second set of doors and across the lobby. She was vaguely aware of the desk clerk, and from what she could tell he didn't even so much as raise an eyebrow to see who had walked in. When they reached his room, she relaxed a little.

Once inside, Beliah locked the door and grinned. She was spellbound. All of her seductive power vanishing in the moment. She had never been in a situation where she felt so totally out of control and loving it. He was just inches from her and the deeper he stared the hotter she became. An animal lust was building within her. She never wanted anyone as much as she wanted him.

"Now I'll make you a woman," he growled.

He snatched her up and threw her down on the bed. He knelt down next to her, straddling her at the waist with his legs, and grabbed her neck with both hands.

The pressure around her neck increased and she started to squirm beneath him. She managed a sound but it was choked off. Missy began to panic. She looked up at him and saw that he was smiling. The looked surprised her and she thought she was in the hands of a sadist. The pressure eased slightly but he didn't let go.

"Missy, sweetheart. Trussst me," he hissed.

She felt helpless under his weight. He released his grip on her neck and lowered his head to her breasts. He bit into her shirt and reared back his head, causing the tee-shirt to tear away from her. He looked down at her—the shirt still clenched between his teeth—and fondled her bare, white breasts with a free hand.

His eyes were glowing red, and he began to change. His nose began to lengthen and his teeth grew into sharpened fangs. What had once been a handsome man was now a hideous beast, more wolf than human.

Her body twisted beneath him in agonizing pleasure, and as he penetrated her she felt him entering her soul, violating that as well as her body. She didn't care anymore. Her body relaxed under his rough caresses and she closed her eyes to whatever was to come. Pain or pleasure, she welcomed it. She was totally under his control and wanted it that way.

6

The desk clerk looked up from watching TV, drawn away by the strange snarling sounds emanating from one of the rooms. He followed the noise over to the door and pressed his ear against it. He heard what sounded like animals and raised his hand to knock. But at the sound of a muffled scream, he shrugged his shoulders and thought, *He's probably got whore in there.* He was smiling brightly as he settled back down in front of the TV.

7

Beliah was ravenous when he left his room. He whistled to himself as he walked to the front desk. "I'll need a maid in my room, if you don't mind."

The man turned to him and gave Beliah a knowing wink. "Mess up the sheets, did you?"

"Don't you know it, man? She's one hot bitch. Here." Beliah handed the man a hundred dollar bill. "Maybe she'll do you."

The man took the bill, smiled, and watched Beliah walk out of the hotel.

Beliah looked across the street at a restaurant on the other side. "Country Cafe" was etched into the large, plate-glass window. He chuckled to himself and walked across the street to the restaurant. Opening the door, he was hit in the face by a blast of hot air. The place was like a sauna. Obviously the proprietor didn't believe in air conditioning. There was a good size crowd dining on pork chops and black-eye peas, and when he entered all conversation stopped. After a quick glance in his direction, the diners returned to their various discussions. All but one: A lone man in a corner booth by the window. He continued to stare at Beliah with a look that resembled hatred and extreme disgust.

Beliah purposely ignored the man and sat in a booth at the other side of the cafe. He picked up the menu and scanned through the selections. It wasn't a minute later that he heard someone approaching. He knew it was the man at the other table and hiked his menu higher to avoid looking at him until he was right on top of Beliah.

The man stopped a few feet short of the table and cleared his throat. Beliah slowly lowered the menu, trying to hold back a smile, and peered up at the tall, thin man. He was wearing what Missy would have said was a "mean man" face. He looked extremely angry.

"Can I help you?" Beliah asked.

"I don't think so you pervert, but I've got a few words of advice for you."

"And what might those be?"

"I thought you were a pervert when I read your book, but now I have proof. I saw you."

"Man, what are you talking about?" Beliah lowered his eyes again and continued to browse the menu selections.

"Missy. I saw you two. Don't try to deny it. I was sittin' right over there when you two ran into the hotel," he spat, pointing a shaking finger at his table.

"Is that so?"

"Y-Yeah, that's so." The look Beliah gave him unnerved him. He fully expected Beliah to dispute the fact. "You must be warped or something. Hell, she's only seventeen. That Missy, she's my boy's girl."

"So your Tommy's father? You must have a heck of a boy to win that one. She's wild. But I wouldn't worry; he won't be able to keep her. Not now. I think I have ruined her for other guys. They won't be able to handle her." The corner of Beliah's mouth twisted up into a sarcastic smile.

"You don't deny it? I'll get you. Not now but later—at the meeting tonight. The whole town will know what you and that slut did."

"You'll be at the meeting tonight? Great! I'll look for you. I'll even share the stage. Do you have a speechwriter? I know a good one."

"What are you?" Tommy's father backed away with fear reflected in his pale blue eyes. "I'm gonna tell the Sheriff. He'll arrest you and lock you up. You're gonna pay." He was close to screaming and his voice cracked under the strain. He backed his way out of the cafe still shouting.

The café grew quiet and the crowd turned to give Beliah an inquisitive, distrustful look.

"I guess he didn't like the book." Beliah shrugged. A couple of the diners laughed at that and returned to their meals.

Go tell the Sheriff, he thought. *You're hysterical enough to have yourself locked up.*

Beliah felt very sure of himself. If there was anything he knew—and he knew a lot—then human nature was it. The Sheriff may question him, but that would be the extent of it. And that would only happen if he found out. Beliah cleared his mind of all thought, allowing him to scan the life forces of the town. He discovered several that he had met and a couple he hadn't. He was looking for something, and when he found it he reached out with his mind and took possession of it.

"Can I get you something to drink?" said a pretty, sweet-talking waitress.

"Sure. How about some coffee?" Beliah smiled at her.

8

In a darken theater in the middle of Main, a young man who worked part-time at the only hotel in town, stared at the screen with a vacant look in his eyes. He felt an icy-cold presence enter into him, taking over his mind. He allowed it for he had no will to stop it. A command was given concerning a man he knew. The man was Tommy's father. The command demanded him to stop Tommy's father.

The young man was released from his mental captivity and blinked several times to clear his head of the fuzzy stupor he had been in. He felt like he was stoned, not knowing where he was or what he was doing, but believed he had something to do, something important, something concerning Tommy's father. A flash of light from the screen brought him fully awake and he was shocked to discover he was in the movie theater watching what, he didn't know. He walked out of the theater without seeing how the movie ended and headed east on Main Street.

He hadn't seen Mr. Richardson in a long time. He knew he owned the gun store, but didn't go in there often. At the end of the block, he stopped in front of a small shop with bars across the door and across the large front window. He stared at the dull, brass knob for a moment before reaching out to open the door. "Mr. Richardson?" he asked.

"I'm in the back," came the strange reply.

9

"I can't believe the crowd here," Jason said as he and Tommy walked up the whitewashed steps of City Hall. "The whole town's here."

"I know. I think I saw Pastor Blanchard. Why do you think he'd come?"

Jason shrugged and reached for the door. A wave of superheated air, generated by the enormous amount of people in the tiny hall, struck them hard with the reminder that summer was on its way. Within seconds, they were both perspiring. The auditorium was filling up rapidly, so they sat down near the back. Jason craned his neck to see who was in the crowd and noticed Pastor Blanchard was indeed in the audience. Why would he be here?

Moments later, a hush grew over the crowd as the man Jason had seen on the back cover of the book strolled across the stage to center. There was no microphone set up. A murmur spread through the audience as they noticed it and realized he would speak to this gathering using the strength of his own voice.

Standing with his hands crossed casually behind his back, Beliah remained quiet and waited until every eye was focused on him. And then waited some more. As the anxiety grew, the audience fidgeted in the uncomfortable silence. Jason wondered if he would ever speak.

And then he did.

"My name is Beliah," he said affectionately. "Welcome! I have missed you. It has been a long time. I must ask of you now the question I asked years before. What is your purpose? You still do not know? Of course you don't. That's why I'm here. I'm here to tell you about your power. I'm here to tell you of your destiny. I hold the key that will unlock your mind and free you of your physical bonds. If you will let me, I will take your hand and guide you through this Hell you've created for yourselves. Together, we will become Master."

The audience started mumbling and Jason took the moment to ask Tommy, "What's he talking about?"

Tommy replied, "You askin' me?"

"To prepare you, you must understand that reality is an illusion. Everything you perceive with your senses is nothing more than mere opinion. Open your mind, for what I am about to tell you will stretch it beyond the limits of this reality.

"The answer to your question is one that I will give you, but first I must warn you that what I'm about to say will go against most of your Christian beliefs. Prepare yourselves, for what I say next may destroy some, and enlighten others. I tell you the truth. Your visions of Heaven and Hell will be shattered." Beliah stopped speaking and smiled to himself.

Jason and Tommy sat staring at each other with their mouths hanging open. They had never heard such ideas as the ones Beliah hinted at. With the arrogance that Beliah had just displayed, there was only one thing that could happen. After a short period of shocked silence, the entire congregation of religious, bible-belt church goers...

"Who the hell do you think you are?"

Exploded!

"How dare you speak such blasphemy?!"

"You're gonna burn in Hell!"

Much to Jason's surprise, Beliah started to laugh. Beliah raised his hand to his mouth to cover the expression, but failed miserably. It was pretty obvious to everyone that he thought the outbursts were funny. This guy's gonna be lynched. Several minutes later the yelling and damning dropped off and people started to leave. Beliah's expression changed to questioning concern and he waved a hand in the air beckoning them to return.

"Before you leave," he said, "why don't you ask your Pastor what he has to say? I will gladly answer any questions he has to offer."

"Yeah, let's hear from Pastor Blanchard," a man sitting just behind Jason said. He recognized the voice and turned around in his seat to see him. The voice belonged to a tall man in his thirty's who was slightly over-weight, with jet-black hair. His name was Jim and he ran the only garage in town.

Jason turned back around and saw Beliah staring at him. A cold chill ran down the length of his back, causing him to sink down in his seat. When Beliah's eyes didn't follow him down, he realized Beliah was looking at Jim.

"I'm glad he's not lookin' at me like that," Jason said.

"What?" Tommy replied.

"His eyes," he said aloud. And then quieter, "What's behind those eyes?" Jason glanced at Jim again and saw the fear he had felt reflected in Jim's eyes. Is Beliah using some kind of spell on him? He was about to whisper Jim's name when Beliah broke the silence.

"Yes, let's hear from Pastor Blanchard."

Pastor Blanchard rose slowly to his feet. The silence in the auditorium was so complete that a small boy in the front row giggled at the sound of Blanchard's arthritic knees popping. He was a man of moderate height and weight with a touch of gray sprinkled throughout his black hair. He looked tired, Jason thought, and unsure of himself.

"If I have offended you," Beliah said, "I would like the opportunity to explain myself."

Blanchard cleared his throat and opened his mouth. When nothing came out, Jason wondered if he was going to break out in song. He didn't and closed his mouth.

Blanchard cleared his throat once again and said, "I don't think I have anything to say to you."

Most of the older people voiced outrage in agreement with his comment and again rose to leave. The temperature of the room increased dramatically and Jason thought they were going to pull Beliah off the stage and crucify him. This man had turned a God-fearing Baptist community into a lynching mob.

Beliah raised both arms in the air and asked, "May I have you attention, please? Please?"

Without any further protest, the auditorium became quiet.

"For those of you who would like more information," Beliah said, "I will have a book signing tomorrow. I'll be more than happy to explain the mystery of life to those who wish to know the truth. This gathering is concluded."

10

Jason and Tommy were the first ones to leave the auditorium. The cool night air felt good after the sizzling hour they had spent inside. Their sweaty clothes clung to them, and within seconds Jason started to get a chill. He put his arms around himself for warmth, and then he noticed a flickering light glowing in the distance. "What's goin' on over there?"

While they had been inside, a fire broke out on the east side of town. Gray and red clouds of smoke floated violently up from one of the buildings on Main Street. Even from this distance, Jason could see the red and blue lights of the emergency vehicles, flashing strobe-like in the dark.

"Idda know," Tommy said. "I didn't hear an explosion or anything. Did you?"

"Uh-uh. Let's go check it out."

As they were leaving, most of the people had managed to exit the auditorium and were asking the same question as Jason. "If we hurry, we can beat the rush," he said.

They ran down Commerce and rounded the corner of Main, breathing heavily. The emergency vehicles were parked on the right at the end of Main. Seeing the location of the parked vehicles, they stopped dead in their tracks. There was only one building it could have been.

"Tommy, was your dad working late tonight?" Jason asked.

"Yeah," he said, and then sprinted towards his father's store.

Jason followed and caught up to him only after they had reached the store. Sheriff Dunn was talking to one of the fire medics when he noticed Jason and Tommy. He walked over to them and Tommy was the first to speak. "What's going on, Sheriff?"

"Tommy," Dunn said, "I've already called your mother and she should be here in a few minutes. I want you to stay here until she arrives."

"But what happened?"

"I can't answer that right now. I just need the two of you to stay out of the way. Do you understand?"

"It's my dad, isn't it? He's hurt. I know he is." Tommy's voice jumped up a couple of octaves and he was on the verge of panic. "I need to see him and make sure he's all right."

"Tommy, I can't let you do that right now. Wait until—"

Tommy bolted past Dunn and headed for the front door. The move took Dunn by surprise and he tripped over his own feet trying to grab him. The Sheriff came down hard on his hip and he suppressed a painful cry.

Jason took the opportunity and darted after Tommy, more afraid of what he might find than disobeying the Sheriff. "Tommy, wait for me."

Jason reached the door of the gun shop and froze. The scene was something out of a cop TV program. The store was scorched from top to bottom by fire. Pieces of broken glass from a shattered gun case lay haphazardly on the floor. As far as he could tell, most of the guns were still there. He carefully stepped across the floor and made his way to the back room. There he gasped and stared in horror at what he saw.

On the desk was a large caliber handgun, a partially broken ashtray and the remains of what looked like a bottle of alcohol. Mr. Richardson was reclining behind the desk in his swivel chair with his head back. He was burnt to a crisp from the waist up—Jason couldn't see his legs under the desk—and he could see that everything on his face from the nose down was gone. Only a few broken teeth remained in the upper plate.

"Let's go boys," Dunn said sadly from behind them.

"My God, S-S-Sheriff," Jason said, tears streaming down his face. "Mr. Richardson's—"

"He's gone. We got here too late. There was nothing we could do."

Jason collapsed on the floor next to Tommy and put his arms around his friend. "I'm sorry, Tommy. Oh God I'm sorry." He looked back at Mr. Richardson's body and found himself almost eye level with the seated dead man.

Dunn knelt down and put his hand lightly on Jason's head. "I need your help to get Tommy out of here. I told the fire medics to wait outside until we come out. Can you do that?"

Jason nodded and stood up. He got on one side of Tommy with Dunn on the other and together they lifted him up. Jason wrapped his arm around Tommy's waist and half guided, half forced him out of the store and into the street. Tommy was in shock and fell to the ground once he was outside. The Fire medics picked him up and carried him to the ambulance where someone injected something into his arm.

Jason staggered across the street and sat down on the curb opposite the store. He saw Mrs. Richardson drive up, practically falling out of her car, and run over to her son. She questioned one of the fire medics treating her son and he pointed into the store. She gave Tommy a kiss on the forehead and fled into the smoked-out remains.

Sheriff Dunn met her at the door, they hugged, and then they disappeared into the smoky darkness. A few moments later a woman screamed and all eyes turned toward the store. The high-pitched scream turned into loud sobbing. Dunn emerged from the store holding Mrs. Richardson in the same manner as Jason had carried out her son.

As the minutes stretched into hours, Jason watched as the crowd grew and then was chased away by the Sheriff. The county coroner showed up a little after ten and spent a good thirty minutes in the store with Dunn. They went in talking and came out later the same way. Dunn nodded his head in response to the questions the coroner asked while the coroner wrote the responses in a little brown book. After walking the coroner to his car, Dunn roped off the area with yellow crime-scene tape. Moments later, the area was sealed and the coroner drove off in the direction of the hospital.

Dunn watched him go and then moved toward Tommy and Mrs. Richardson. Jason repositioned himself within earshot, hoping that Dunn would answer some of his own questions.

"Mrs. Richardson," Dunn said, "I'm very sorry."

"Thank you, Sheriff. Could you please tell me what happened?"

Jason was surprised by her courage. She didn't even seem to be upset.

"I think it would be best if the boy—"

"The boy is fine. It'd be better if he heard the truth from you than heard it through the grapevine." Mrs. Richardson looked at her son, noticing that the medicine the medics gave him put him in a slight stupor, but he was calm and that's what mattered right now.

Dunn nodded in agreement. "Of course. I just meant it might be painful. I wanted to protect him."

"Sheriff, his father is dead. How can you protect him from that?"

"I'm sorry. As far as we can tell, it was an accident, or more accurately, a series of tragic events. The county coroner is under the impression that your husband died because of an accidental discharge of a pistol. Flames caused by a combination of alcohol and cigarettes covered the handgun on his desk, and the heat of the fire set it off. He took the round in the mouth."

"Then it wasn't a suicide?"

"I don't think so. Judging by the location of the gun in relation to his hands, well... I don't think it was."

Mrs. Richardson seemed to breathe a sigh of relief, and then she broke down again. Tommy closed his eyes and lowered his head. Tears flowed down the side of his face. After a minute or so Mrs. Richardson said, "You said something about alcohol and cigarettes?"

"Yes. It appears he was having a drink while..."

"Sheriff, my husband doesn't, I mean, didn't drink."

"I don't doubt you Mrs. Richardson. I'm just trying to give you the facts of the matter. There was an empty bottle of Rum found on his desk."

"I see."

"Yes. He must have fallen asleep while smoking and at some point spilled the liquor. His cigarette ignited the alcohol and..."

Jason couldn't listen any more, he had heard enough. He stood and shoved his hands deep into his pockets. A cool wind blew down Main and he shivered. The chill reminded him of Beliah. He didn't think one had anything to do with the other, but still he wondered. The moment Beliah was stirring up trouble in the auditorium, Tommy's dad was getting half of his face blown off. The thought, more than the wind, left him cold.

CHAPTER 3

The greatest fear man must face is the fear of himself. Only when he faces this fear will his true character emerge.
From The Book of Beliah
Verse 19

11

BELIAH SMILED MISCHIEVOUSLY TO HIMSELF. Everything was going perfectly. That boy Tommy would be another recruit: Child's play. There was a slight breeze blowing and it felt good on his face. A scrap of paper tumbled down the street and he put his foot on it to stop it. He reached down and picked it up. He laughed while he read, understanding the importance of what he read. It was the church bulletin. It stated: Truth is the opening of doors, the revealing of secrets, the shroud that has been removed from our eyes. Truth is a spiritual awakening!

Yeah right, he thought. *What is truth?* Then in a whisper, "I will give them all the truth they will ever need."

Beliah turned away from the gun store and looked west down Main Street. He really didn't feel like going back to his room—torn between his joy at seeing the carnage and his disappointment with the pastor—but began walking in the direction of the hotel anyway. *Blanchard had given in too soon,* he thought. There was always a moral leader, someone for whom Beliah could cast as the bad guy. Now, someone else might turn up, someone who hadn't been at the meeting. That would complicate things a bit. If it turned out to be someone he hadn't seen, then the impact of the meeting would have been a waste.

Most people deep in thought would not have noticed the buildings lining the street. As it was, Beliah was aware of everything, even when it seemed impossible to notice details. As he walked, he made a mental note of all the storefronts, even down to the items displayed in the windows. There was the auto parts store directly across the street from the gun store. They were having a sale tomorrow and for the rest of the week to clear out inventory.

Next to the auto parts store was a grocery store. He noticed one lone vehicle in the parking lot. It was a red Chevy pickup with Florida tags. Beliah reminded himself to find out if the owner was truly from out of town or just a lazy son-of-a-bitch who didn't feel like he had to change his tags over. The run-down movie theater across the street from the grocery was playing "Natural Born Killers". The theater was sandwiched between the gun store and a video store that advertised "Two rentals, two nights, two bucks!"

The vacant lot on the right hand side of the street ran between the grocery store and Jim's garage. In back of that was a large, wooded lot filled with pecan trees.

Beliah stopped at the intersection of Main and Commerce. He paused in his thoughts and looked left, south down Commerce. City Hall was located at the end of the street, and also the auditorium where just a few hours ago most of the town had collected to hear what he had to say. He turned his head to the right and at that end of the street he could see the church. It was partially obscured by a large, rundown water fountain. He understood completely the law concerning separation of church and state, but this was ridiculous. *Soon,* he thought, *this town will know why the founding fathers had thought it wise to include that clause in their worthless piece of law.*

"What's goin' on down there?" an obviously drunk man asked. He staggered towards Beliah and stopped abruptly, reeking of alcohol and piss.

"There seems to have been a shooting at the gun store," Beliah said.

"At Richardson's place?"

"I don't know who owns the place, but I'm sure you're right."

"Well, I'll be damned!"

"Yes, you will."

"What?"

"Nothing, my man. Say! You seemed to be doing just what I wish I was doing right about now."

"What?" the man said again.

"Drinking my man; partaking of the spirits."

"Dri... Well shore! That's where I just come from. Sandy's place is at the end of the street."

"Man, if you mean the local bar, then by all means… Show me the way."

"But Richardson's..."

"Man, you can read about it in the paper tomorrow. It is all over except for the crying. Come on! Let me buy you a drink. What's your name?"

"Willy. And okay, as long as you're buyin'."

"Man, you'll never have to buy a drink again." Beliah put his arm around the stinking man's shoulders and together they headed down the street to Sandy's.

Beliah stepped into Sandy's Bar ahead of Willy. The door opened inward and Beliah took the place in at a glance. It was very typical of any small town bar. Directly in front of him were three square tables spread out in a triangle formation; the right side wall having two tables with the third centered and equally spaced away from the other two. A forth table was off to his left side sitting in front of the only window in the place. The window faced south and Beliah thought that even in the middle of day, it would still be dark. The TV in the front left corner of the building was turned to some News channel.

"Get you a seat," Willy said as he pushed Beliah aside; he then made a beeline toward the woman behind the bar.

Willy sat down at the small bar with a plop, the old, four-legged stool creaking under the strain. He was a large man only because of his gut, a shape he worked to enhance everyday doing 12 oz. curls. His thinning blond hair was unkempt and laid wildly about his head. It was pretty easy to see he was a regular by the nonchalant manner in which he sat at the bar.

"Hey Willy," the woman behind the mahogany bar said. "Who's the new guy?"

"Well sweetheart," Beliah said sitting down next to Willy, "names are unimportant. What is important is that I promised my friend here a drink. In fact, I'm buying the house a round." A slight howl of agreement erupted from the few other customers in the bar.

"Sure mister. What'll ya have?"

"Give him what I'm having Wanda," Willy said, reaching over the bar and pulling back a Miller Lite. "Be easy on 'em. He's from out of town." He bulldozed his hand into the bowl of pretzels sitting on the bar and proceeded to stuff them in his mouth.

Wanda pulled three Miller's and a Miller Lite from a small refrigerator under the bar. She popped the caps and grabbed a bottle of Jack Daniel's.

Beliah watched her from behind as she measured out a shot of "Jack". His eyes glided over her body and stopped at the beautiful shape hanging between her waist and thighs. *Lovely,* he thought. *Such a perfect shape. And still firm, too.* Beliah thought of her bent over a stool with him deep inside her, although there was nothing sexual about it. He wanted to rip her apart and watch her squirm in pain. Suddenly, he caught his reflection in the back mirror and it made him smile. *That mirror will come in handy. She will see me and I can see the look on her face.*

12

Wanda turned around and saw Beliah staring at her. She was use to that. Ever since she started working in bars she had to deal with drunks making passes at her, mostly bad ones at that. Sometimes she would let them pick her up. Hell, she had needs just like everybody, and if some cute guy from out of town came in she'd giv'em a roll in the sack. Nothing wrong with that, she thought. She returned Beliah's stare and he didn't flinch. Instead, he grinned and winked at her. Oddly, she felt this overwhelming need to pounce on him right then and there. She tried to shake the feeling, but couldn't, or wouldn't, do it.

"Where's my drink?" someone shouted.

That did it. Jolted back to the here and now, she noticed Beliah had disappeared. The door to the bathroom was closing and she saw the back of one leg entering the stall. What had she been staring at? "I'm getting your damn drink, Earl. Now wait a minute," she shouted to the costumer in the back corner by the bathroom.

The bathroom door opened a few minutes later and a renewed stench filled the air. It had the smell of raw sewage, but no one seemed to notice. Beliah walked out and clapped his hand on the back of the man who had hollered for his booze. "Hey man, haven't you received your drink yet?"

"Ah… that bitch. She's slower than my grandma, God rest her soul."

"I'm sure he has."

"Huh?"

"Hey Wanda," Beliah said. "Bring this man his whiskey and make it two. I'll drink it over here."

Wanda served the two men at the far end of the bar their beers and loaded a tray with the remaining drinks. She lifted the tray shoulder high and slid between the bar stools and the third table in the group of three.

She set the Miller Lite down at the table by the window and started towards the third table. As she turned, the man sitting at the window table smacked her on the ass. She thought nothing of it. She knew him well, very well. She set down the last beer and moved to the back corner table.

"There you are gentlemen," she said setting the drinks down, all the while watching Beliah.

"Thanks, Wanda. I can call you Wanda, can't I?" Beliah asked, handing her a hundred dollar bill, which seemingly materialized out of thin air between his two raised fingers.

"Honey, if you can do that all night," she said, taking the bill out of his hand, "you can call me yours."

Wanda threw back her head, laughing, her long, crimson hair falling about her face and neck. Her large brown eyes had a spirited look that most men found seductive, and she used it to her advantage. But that look didn't work on Beliah. Instead, that feeling of lust once again warmed her loins, making her feel slightly queasy and light-headed. Just look away, she told herself, but this time was no different than the first. Her smile vanished from her face and was replaced by desire. She parted her lips and moistened them with her thick, soft tongue, uncontrollably aware of the hunger growing in her belly and down her thighs. "I want…"

"Wanda, what the Sam hell's wrong with you tonight?" It was Willy. "I've been hollerin' at you. We're all out of Miller!"

"I… It's… I've got some more in the back. Just sit down. Can't you see I'm talking to Mister…?"

"It looks to me more like you're in heat. Wipe your mouth and c'mon," Willy yelled.

Wanda wiped her mouth with the back of her hand and looked at it. She had been drooling, or more to the point, slobbering.

"I think you should go get his beer," Beliah said.

"Yeah, I'll do that, but don't you go away. I'll be right back." Wanda turned and left. *What's the matter with me*, she thought. *He must think I'm a whore.* Then from somewhere in the back of her mind she heard a voice that said, "You will indeed be my whore!" She let out a startled yelp and looked back at him. He was busy talking to Earl. She shrugged but couldn't shake the feeling that he had spoken to her without saying a word. She walked toward the back, reaching for the walk-in refrigerator and pulled on the handle. The large, thick door swung open and revealed a chilled interior filled with beer and unprepared bar food. She heard Willy yell again for his beer. Wanda reached for a case of Miller longnecks and said, "I'm coming, you asshole!"

She hoisted the case of beer onto her shoulder and realized it was missing a couple of six packs. The case shifted and she lost her footing on the slick floor, falling against a rack full of loose beers. The impact made one of the bottles topple over, breaking at the neck, pouring forty-degree brew down the front of her pants. "Damn!"

13

"That's a strong drink for a man drinking alone," Beliah said. "Especially a man with the troubles you have." He raised the glass to his lips and downed it in one swallow.

"Mister, thanks for the drink, but my problems ain't any of your business." Earl swallowed his shot and then said, "Besides, what you know of them?"

Beliah leaned forward and lowered his voice to a whisper. "I know a great deal. I make it my business to know."

"Yeah, says you. Look, I just want to be alone. Do you mind?"

Beliah studied the man before him. Earl was a man of about fifty years. His gray hair had a light blue sheen that contrasted with his black-as-night face. The lines across his forehead spoke of years locked in deep thought, most of those years clouded in a dark vale of hatred and bitterness. His large nose was set between ample cheeks and it looked like it had been broken a time or two: it pointed in two different directions at once. His runny eyes suggested he drank more than he ate.

Beliah leaned back in his chair. *This man,* he thought, *has a lot of pain. Perfect.* The noise level in the bar picked up and Beliah raised his voice so he could be heard. "No, I don't mind. I just think a black man living in the South sure has it tough."

"What do you know 'bout it?"

"Quite a bit, I should say. My grandfather was born in the South and it just so happens he was a man of color."

Wanda brought a bottle of "JD" over to the table and Beliah said, "Leave it, Wanda. I think we're gonna finish that up."

Earl eyeballed Beliah as he spoke, never once looking at Wanda. She set the bottle down and left. Earl snatched it up and refilled the glasses to the top. He downed his shot in one fluid motion and set the glass down hard on the table.

"So that makes you an expert on black people then?" Earl reached in his shirt pocket for a pack of cigarettes and offered one to Beliah.

Beliah declined and said, "I wouldn't say expert, but my grandfather was strung up by a couple of rednecks a few years ago. He was running for city council and they thought he was getting too popular for his own good."

Earl looked hard at Beliah and decided he liked him. He studied his face, and what he once thought of as long flowing blonde hair now had a darker, more curled appearance. Beliah's forehead was more prominent and his lips seemed fuller, too. "You know what? I can see the black in you. I like that in a man." They both laughed and Earl thought he had found a kindred soul.

14

Jason couldn't believe what had happened. Tommy's father was dead. Just like that. He didn't know what to think. What do you say to a guy who just lost their father, especially like that? Did stuff like that happen all by itself? He didn't think so.

Jason watched as Tommy and his mother drove away in the ambulance heading to the hospital. Tommy seemed to be holding up reasonably well, that is if you call staring off into space and looking like a zombie reasonably well. Jason turned to go. There was nothing left for him to do and he felt alone and helpless. His house was down Lee Street, heading north out of town. There were two ways of getting there. If he were driving, Lee Street would have been the logical choice, but since he was on foot he turned west and headed down Main Street.

Jason rounded the corner of the grocery store and passed through a vacant lot between the grocery store and Jim Langley's garage. Behind the store the lot opened up into a forest of trees. Jason knew these woods better than anyone. The woods covered 25 acres that were jointly owned by the church and the city council. That went against the law but was the only solution to a problem that Jason really didn't know about or even cared to. As far as he was concerned those woods belonged to him and all the other kids that played in them.

He entered the woods and stopped at a large, old tree that served as a boundary marker between the town and the woods. On it he saw the names of hundreds of kids, most now grown old and some that had died, permanently carved into the husk of the tree.

He ran his finger across the rough, textured surface and outlined his own engraved name. Tommy's name was to the left of his and he remembered the day they had carved them. Tears welled up in his eyes. Childhood was truly over for Jason now. He knew the world could be a terrible place, but he had somehow been protected from it. The death hit home. Why did something like that have to happen? Jason left the tree and continued down a path that had been worn away by years of travel.

Except for a light barely visible through the trees, Jason was in complete darkness. Ordinarily, the dark wouldn't have bothered him. Walking through these woods at night was as natural to him as lying in his own bed. But tonight, just as things can lurk under your bed, Jason had the unnerving feeling that he was being watched. He slowed his pace and nervously glanced around. Nothing was there. He buried his hands deep into his faded blue-jean pockets, hunched his shoulders and quickened his step. He knew that the events of tonight were bothering him, but he couldn't shake the odd feeling he was being watched.

After about twenty minutes, Jason emerged from the woods. Lee Street stretched out in front of him. His house was on the other side of the road and down a short gravel drive. It was dark, except for a front porch light. He walked around to the back of the house and a dog met him at the fence. "Shh, boy, it's just me."

Jason loved his dog. Most people were afraid of him, but Jason thought of him as one big puppy. Tonka was a mutt, part hound, part boxer, and weighed somewhere around 100 pounds. Fawn in color, his black muzzle tended to draw most of the attention. He had a head as big as a basketball and a mouth to go along with it. Jason could see why most people feared him.

Tonka stood on his hind legs and rested his front paws on top of the four-foot high fence. Jason playfully slapped him across the side of the head. The dog growled and then panted. Jason patted his head and said, "Good Boy!"

Tonka barked in agreement.

"Let's go inside, boy. Jump!"

The dog sat down and then lunged over the fence in a single bound. He landed on all fours and trotted after Jason, stopping once, smelling the scent of an interloper and then marking his territory.

Around front Jason found the door unlocked, as always. Living in a small town has it advantages. Of course, with a dog like Tonka around Jason doubted if anyone would be senseless enough to try and break in. He didn't know if Tonka would actually bite anyone or not, but a would-be thief might find himself licked to death.

Jason opened the door and found a note lying on the front steps. It was from his mother. It read:

Hi honey,

Went to see if there was anything I could do for Mrs. Richardson. Your father went to the police station to see what he could find out. There's sandwich meat in the ice box. I haven't fed Tonka. Sorry! See you soon.

Love ya,
Mom

Jason folded the note in half and then ripped it in two. He loved his mom, but he also knew the main reason she went to Tommy's house was to get some juicy gossip. In her world, "She who holds the best gossip is the one who rules."

His father, on the other hand, was always trying to get in the middle of things. An avid detective novel reader, his father thought he knew more than the police and was certain he could do a better job. "After all," he could hear his father say, "I always solve the crime before the last chapter."

His father did have his own opinions about things and on more than one occasion he had turned out to be right. But this, he thought, was a real death. Nothing made up about it. The town would be in chaos over this. Everyone would be involved.

Jason opened a can of dog food and put it in Tonka's bowl. "Sit!" he said, and Tonka did as he was told. Drool collected at the corners of the dog's mouth and Jason smiled. As hungry as he knew his dog was he knew Tonka would stay there indefinitely if need be. He was a very smart and obedient dog. The drool hung down three to four inches from the corner of his mouth in one unbroken string. The dog licked his muzzle and the string disappeared. A few seconds later, the drool reappeared, hanging lower than before.

Raising a pointed finger high in the air Jason said, "Get it, boy!" and quickly brought his finger down, pointing to the bowl. Tonka devoured the meaty-like substance, snorting as he swallowed, without chewing. *I'd hate to be on the wrong end of that mouth if he were really hungry,* Jason thought.

He opened the refrigerator, pulled out a yellow carbonated drink and went into the living room. The memory of Beliah and the meeting was just that, a memory. It seemed to Jason like it was days ago and not, looking at the clock on the wall, three hours ago. The things Beliah said were no longer vivid in his mind. Those things were being filed away to his subconscious while the scene inside the gun store burned an indelible impression on his soul. It fed on his pain and fear and returned him to thoughts about his dreams. The Dark Thing! Jason shivered and the name, Beliah, popped into his mind, but not in connection with the meeting. He saw in his mind's eye a face on the Dark Thing of the night before. The face he saw was Beliah's.

15

"Damn, son. You drink like a fish," Earl said squeezing the last of the Jack into his glass.

Beliah had spent most of the night getting Earl drunk and he knew he was well on his way to a hangover. The alcohol, however, didn't seemed to have any effect on Beliah. He maintained his same relaxed manner while Earl became sloppy and incoherent.

"Hey man, we seem to be out of Jack," Beliah said, reaching for the empty bottle. "I'll get another bottle."

He strolled over to the bar like a man walking a tight wire; his step didn't have a shake or wobble to it. In the time that Beliah had spent getting

Earl inebriated, the bar had cleared out. Willy left an hour ago and took Phil and his friend Jeff with him. The only people left in the bar besides Beliah and Earl were Wanda and the man that had been sitting at the window table, Kevin.

Kevin had moved to the bar and was talking to Wanda when Beliah walked up. Wanda was trying to convince Kevin to leave, but he just didn't want to.

"Fine, then. If you want me to leave so much, then the hell with you. I got better things to do anyway." Kevin was red in the face, mostly from alcohol but also from anger.

"Baby," she said, "I just don't know when I'll be out of here and I see no reason for you to stay. I'll see you tomorrow." She leaned over the bar and grabbed his shirt. "Baby, I'll make it up to you, I promise." She kissed his ear and ran her fingers through his thick wavy hair.

He said, "You better."

Beliah watched the exchange without watching. She was playing that poor jerk like a card, he thought. He liked this woman. If it weren't for that "damned good streak" running through her, he wouldn't mind her joining him. As it was, she would have to die. Beliah smiled as he watched her lean over the bar. Her full breasts hung down just touching the surface of the bar; her hair falling down her back pointed towards her posterior. Beliah admired her easily worn beauty and thought of her in different, highly sexual positions. *I'll have to wear that out before I kill her,* he thought.

Kevin stumbled out of the bar as Beliah watched him go. He then turned his attention back on Wanda. "Hey Wanda. We need another bottle."

"You goin' to drink that all by yourself?" she said, moving to the other end of the bar.

"Of course not." Beliah hiked his thumb in the direction of Earl. He was acting slightly intoxicated on her account. No one, but no one drank two fifths of Jack and asked for a third without feeling a little drunk. "I'm going to drink it with Earl."

Earl was face down on the table. If it wasn't for the snoring, Wanda might have assumed he was dead. "I don't think Earl wants any more."

Looking over his shoulder Beliah said, "Maybe you're right. I guess since I got him in that condition, I should make sure he gets home."

"No problem. I'll call a cab. I've done it before."

"Great. I'll make sure he gets there okay."

"You can't... I mean you don't have to do that," Wanda said, hoping Beliah would stay. "I've seen him in worst shape."

"But I wouldn't feel right just throwing him into a cab like that. Besides, I know you want to get home to your boyfriend."

"You mean Kevin? He's just a friend. Besides, I wasn't planning on closing just yet, anyway."

"I see. I'll tell you what. I'll take Earl home and come back here. If you're still open, I'll buy you a drink. It's the least I can do for a woman who has taken such good care of me tonight." Another hundred-dollar bill materialized in his hand just like before.

"Oh! I can't take that. You didn't use up all of the last one."

"Then put it on my account because I'm sure I'll be back."

She took the bill, thanked him and called a cab. After hanging up, she poured him another drink and slid it to him. "I'll be right back," she said and went into the back room.

The cab came and Beliah went outside to tell the driver he wasn't needed. He slipped the cabbie a twenty and sent him on his way. Earl, in the meantime, managed to pick himself up and stagger to the bathroom. Beliah went in to relieve himself and saw Earl fighting with his zipper.

"Come on, Earl. Let me take you home."

"I canth... it's sthuck."

"That's quite all right. No one will see you. That, I can promise you."

With that, Beliah put his hand on Earl's shoulder and led him out of the bathroom, out of the bar and into the street. He looked to the end of the street and back. The police had finished their work at the gun store leaving Main deserted. There was a slight chill in the air and Beliah found it refreshing. He knew that the cabbie would never be able to remember who paid him off. In fact, come tomorrow that same cabbie will think he did drop Earl off and got a good tip to boot.

"Ah, the human mind. What a wonderful piece of garbage, don't you think Earl?"

"Whaa?"

"Never mind. Just come with me. I have a surprise for you."

"A slurpise?" Earl's eyes were bloodshot and glazed over.

"Yes. C'mon." Beliah led Earl past the print shop and into the hotel parking lot. The lot was empty except for a few cars. Beliah noticed a red pickup, the same as before. *Ah! A fellow Traveler,* he thought.

They rounded the back of the hotel and came to a grove of trees. "Where are we goin'?" Earl asked.

"None of your business prick!" The tone of his voice was full of hate and Beliah's appearance started to change. He was no longer the dark complexioned man that Earl thought he was. Instead, Beliah's face twisted into a demonic caricature of his former self. His lips were stretched over rotted teeth and his eyes were wide and circular, partially obscured by huge doughy cheeks. His nose was stretched long and curved down over a pointed chin.

"What the hell?"

"Hell is right." Beliah pushed Earl hard and sent him sprawling head first into a tree. "Hey, it's nothing personal, Earl. It's just that, well, I need to feed."

The impact with the tree knocked Earl to the ground. He looked up to see an upside down creature smiling at him. "Oh my God," he croaked.

"Not quite, but close. Now if you don't run I might make it easier on you."

Earl tried to get to his feet but only succeeded in falling back down.

"No need to grovel, Earl. We're friends, remember?" Beliah's arms hung down to his knees, his fingers ending in rapier-like claws.

Earl managed to get to his knees. "P-P-Please, mister, I have a wife and kids. They need me."

"I need you." Beliah drove his claws into Earl's belly and jerked upward, slicing him open like a paper shredder. His guts spilled out across Beliah's feet.

"Pl-"

"Sorry, ole buddy." Beliah stuck out two fingers and said, "You ever see the three stooges do this?" He jabbed his fingers into Earl's eyes, scooping out the two fleshy orbs, leaving nothing but two bloody sockets. "I guess not."

Beliah let go of the lifeless body and it collapsed to the ground. He knelt down and buried his face in the belly of the carcass. He sucked on the intestines as he inserted his hand into the chest cavity. Following a popping sound, he produced the heart. He closed his fingers around it and blood ran down the length of his hairy arm. He brought his hand to his mouth and smeared the bloody muscle all over his face, laughing.

A couple of miles across town Tonka started to growl.

"Shhh… it's okay boy. Go back to sleep," Jason whispered, patting his dog. Tonka lay down but didn't sleep for the rest of the night.

16

"Terrible, it's just terrible. I can't believe it happened." Doris Blanchard closed the front door after escorting the last of the ladies out. "Did you hear what Cathy said about Mr. Richardson's drinking problem?"

Pastor Blanchard was half listening to his wife. Doris and her lady friends had spent most of the night discussing the accident. Those discussions centered on extra-marital affairs, alcoholism and even "possible drug connections." In other words, gossip! His wife was the source of most of the local gossip, whether it was the recent accident or bad-mouthing Wanda Pritchard.

Blanchard knew Wanda was no angel and had his own run-ins with her over the bar. But in spite of her problems he knew she was a woman who had a strong sense of what was right, even if she didn't always follow her own good judgment. In fact, it was that same sagacity that their disagreements centered. She had told him that even though she didn't go to church, that didn't mean she didn't believe. She felt that the whole point of religion was forgiveness. All she had ever encountered, though, was judgment.

"Didn't Jesus die for my sins?" she had asked him.

"Of course," he had replied.

"Then that's good enough for me. He forgave me for my sins, why can't the church?"

How could he argue against that? The people are changing, he thought. There use to be a time when everyone went to church because that was what you did. Now, people have become disillusioned by the church. The answer the church has does not address the problems of today. Too many people were being led astray by false doctrines, like the one tonight. He knew he should have said something. Beliah! That name stuck in his head and he wondered where had he heard it before?

Blanchard adjusted his recliner all the way back. It was getting very late, but he didn't feel sleepy. He looked at the Bible resting on the table next to him. Beliah? Had he read that name in there? He looked above the TV to the bookshelf. There he saw a concordance to the Bible. It was sandwiched between: A History Of God, by Karen Armstrong, and The Oxford Companion to the Bible.

"Mark! Have you been listening to me?" Doris wanted to know.

"Yes, dear." Mark Blanchard sometimes thought that the Catholics had it right by not allowing their priests to marry. Mark loved his wife, but sometimes he deplored her intrusion into his thoughts.

"As I was saying, it seems to me that Mr. Langley is the brains behind the drugs. I never did trust him."

"I know you didn't, but that's no reason to try, convict, and condemn a man." Blanchard normally wouldn't stand up to his wife, not that he was afraid of her, but more to the point that he didn't like to get drawn into her web of conspiracy. She thought everyone had a secret. But tonight, after all that had gone on, he just had to. He liked Jim Langley, although he didn't think Jim knew that.

"Well, then where did he get all of the money to open his garage? I talked to Hillary at the bank and she says he didn't need a loan. In fact, he has seventy-five thousand—"

"Doris, that's enough! I don't want to hear another word. What Hillary did was illegal. She just can't go into any account she wants and then blab to whomever will listen. She could lose her job, or worst." Blanchard got up from his chair. He was mad. Ordinarily, he would let something like that pass. He knew very well what Doris and her ladies did. As bad as it was, he always looked the other way. At least it kept her busy. But tonight, he was on pins and needles. Not so much the accident, but Beliah. Who was he?

"Don't you dare tell a soul—I'm warning you." Doris picked her large frame up off the couch and waddled into the kitchen. She was pushing three hundred pounds with no end sight. "I've worked hard earning the trust of the people in this town. I don't need you to mess it up." She opened the freezer and reached for a pint of chocolate chip cookie dough ice cream.

"Don't worry, sweetheart. I wouldn't think of destroying your standing in the community. Besides, I'm bound by my duty as your pastor not to divulge any confession you might make." With that, Blanchard stormed out of the room.

17

Jason "awoke" to find himself in the middle of a dream. Actually, he was a spectator in his own dream. At first he thought he was watching a movie, but then realized he was part of the surroundings. He tried to interact with the image he saw in front of him and without warning he was pulled into the scene. He felt a slight buzzing sensation and then an incredible surge of energy. He was no longer in the dream but in his own bedroom. He felt a release and then a floating, flowing feeling.

He heard a female voice, but not with his ears. He heard it on a different level of hearing, something beyond sound. It was clearer and more direct. When the voice spoke, it was with such simplicity and yet so much meaning that he knew instinctively he wasn't alone.

"This is how it is," the voice said.

Jason was overwhelmed with the impressions he was receiving. He wanted to meet the owner of that voice, but just as soon as she spoke the feeling that she was there was gone. He was all alone in a world outside of the physical/material realm and yet still part of it. He was floating six inches above his body and knew that the slightest movement in the room would cause him to blow away like a balloon in the wind. He drifted away from his body and over the edge of his bed, conforming to the angle that the bed made with the floor.

Abruptly, he stopped moving. He felt caught. Jason's "eyes" followed the length of his new form up to the top of the bed and saw what had caused him to stop moving. His ethereal feet were still connected to his body. With some effort he floated straight up and stopped, staring at his body lying below him. He still couldn't let go of his feet.

To the left of his bed Tonka was breathing heavily. He tried to call out to him, but discovered he had no voice. He tried again, and then heard something. It wasn't coming from his ethereal body, but from his physical body. Strange! He began to think of his body more like a possession than who he really was.

He tried to call out for the third time and the figure on the bed emitted a sound. It was more of a groan than anything else, a wheezing. The sound was clearer but still not perfect.

Jason realized he was winded. Obviously, breathing by remote control took a lot of energy. The buzzing sensation, which had been with him the whole time, was weaker now. He inhaled and noticed his bodily chest expand. He held that breath for a moment and then let it out. The chest collapsed. The buzzing feeling was as strong as ever. Using all his will, he directed the power of his mind at his body and screamed, "Tonka!"

His body moaned the two-syllable name. His dog jumped, startled awake, and stood looking at Jason's body. He sniffed it and then lay back down. *Amazing,* Jason thought. The dog didn't even notice him floating at the end of the bed. He looked visible enough to him, if not solid, but why couldn't Tonka see him? Weren't dogs supposed to have the ability to sense things that people can't?

He decided against trying to speak again. He learned a lot. He knew if need be he could control his body in his presence form and also that the simple act of breathing energized him. Fine, but how could he release himself from his feet?

"Release your fear of the unknown. Let go." It was that same female voice.

Jason spun around to see where the voice was coming from and completed a three hundred sixty degree turn. When he was facing front again, he looked down at his feet and saw his ghostly legs had twisted around themselves. He felt himself smile and looked at his body. His face carried the smile.

What had the voice said? Release your fear and let go. Jason thought about that. Was he really out of his body as those books said or was this just some weird dream like Tommy thought? Jason didn't know. All he knew was that if this was a dream, it was unlike any he'd ever had, and he was a big-time dreamer. Maybe he *was* afraid of the unknown. This just seemed so natural, though. Almost as if it was a faculty everyone had but didn't know how to use.

He pushed with his mind. "Go!" Gradually, he saw his form pull away from his body, felt a wrenching in his head, almost a tearing away, and then intense pain. The pain felt like a migraine, but all over. He looked at his face and saw the pinched discomfort reflected there. *That looks about as bad as I feel.*

Then, suddenly, the pain stopped. He was free and the mental force he used to overcome his captivity shot him to the ceiling. He felt like a helium balloon that had lost its tether. He kept bouncing around the ceiling without any control.

He realized he no longer looked anything like his body, but was a bluish, smoky, radiant sphere. How he knew this he did not know. He seemed to be able to see all around at once and have that reflected back at him. He could see himself as a ball in the corner of his ceiling and see the room from that perspective at the same time.

Jason thought of his dog and the thought carried him to his dog's side. There was no feeling of movement: first there and now, here. *How did I move?* He decided to try that again, only this time outside his room. He pictured his living room exactly as he had seen it a thousand times before. Again, in the twinkling of an eye, he was there viewing the room from the perspective that he had imagined it. *This is incredible.*

"Go back," the voice said. "You are in danger! Return to the safety of your room."

The words were more like images relaying their meaning directly to his soul. Each word had a visual connotation, and when he "heard" the word danger there was no mistaking it. He was instantly afraid. He tried to envision the layout of his room but couldn't. Fear enslaved his mind. He was in a near panic. Terror overwhelmed him. He didn't know why he should be afraid, only that he was. He tried to move his ethereal form with his mind like before but now he lacked the focus.

Then without warning the room became permeated with a thick, malignant fog. It was of the same consistency as him, but much larger and darker. Where he was blue in color, this Being was coal black. This cloud of terror moved and expanded, filling every corner in the room. It was moving towards Jason at an almost leisurely pace but there was no denying its intent: it was coming for him.

Jason was buzzing fiercely now and wondered if it was possible if he could explode. He felt his Being emit tiny wisps of energy in the form of tentacles. They drifted with a mind of their own, seeking a way of escape.

The cloud was all around him now. It moved forward and then drifted back, bouncing off his sphere of energy. Each contact caused him to realize that he was weakening. The black cloud moved in closer and absorbed more of the impact. Jason's essence shrank to the size of a baseball, solidifying as he got smaller. As the cloud closed in on him, he felt his life was about to be extinguished.

In a last ditch effort he tried to visualize his room again. It wasn't a vivid representation, but it was his room nonetheless. One of his tentacles had found his body and attached itself to his forehead. He had a direct link with his body again, but instead of wanting to be released from it he wanted nothing more than to join it. Once he had formulated that desire in his mind, the action was taken.

"You can't get away that easy, boy," a dark voice boomed.

Jason was surprised to find that he could hear with his ears but that the sound didn't wake his dog. He was caught between two realities, the physical/material and wherever his gaseous self was.

"You learn quick, boy." It was the Dark Thing of the night before, he was sure of it.

Jason thought of his dog. Obviously, the sound he heard was only mental stimulation. If he could moan as before, maybe he could wake his dog. Jason felt that was all that was needed to fully integrate himself back into his body, just some form of connection with the physical. He began to moan.

"That's okay, boy. I've got the rest of your life to get you."

"Waaaaaaaah!" Jason was screaming. "Helllllllp! Don't let him get me. Stop!" Jason sat up in bed, fully awake.

The lights flicked on. "Jason, you okay?" It was his mother.

"Y-Y-Yeah, mom. I'm fine. It was just a bad dream."

"I'll say. You woke up the whole house, probably the neighbors as well."

"I know. I'm sorry. You can go back to sleep."

"Are you going to be okay?"

"Yeah. Go on back to sleep. Could you leave the light on, though? I think I'm going to read for awhile, try to clear my head."

"Okay. Sleep tight. Don't let the bed bugs bite." His mother smiled at him.

"I think they already have." They both laughed. Funny now, but Jason wouldn't sleep for the rest of the night.

CHAPTER 4

Our eyes see only a limited range of light. Our ears hear a certain range of sound. This reality is only one frequency of combined perception.
From The Book of Beliah
Verse 31

18

WANDA OPENED THE DOOR AND looked down Main Street. It was dead quiet. "Damn!" she said aloud. She closed the door and flipped over the open sign. She stopped, hesitated, and flipped it over again. "Damn, damn!"

She was more frustrated with herself than anything else. So she was stood up. So what? She had been stood up before. The guy would promise to come back later in the night only to be too drunk to find his way back. This guy—she still didn't know his name—was probably too drunk to make it. Hell, after all, he did help finish off two bottles of whiskey. Truthfully, she was surprised he could walk, much less carry on a conversation. He had probably dropped Earl off at home and then went to the hotel.

He said he was in town for business and Wanda toyed with the idea of going over there. She laughed to herself. That would definitely make her look like she was a whore. He would more than likely whip out another hundred. She thought about that for a moment: Three hundred dollars for two bottles of whiskey and a roll in the hay? Not a bad idea. That was more than she made in a week. She snorted. There were some things even she wouldn't do. Flirt, yes. Bop some guy in front of his house while his wife and kids were fast asleep inside, sure. But getting laid for money wasn't on her list of things to try. *The hell with him,* she thought. She turned the sign back around and flicked out the lights.

What really made her mad was the fact that she blew off Kevin. He really was a sweet guy, even if he did beat her occasionally. She had been beaten before, and probably would again. Although with Kevin the beatings weren't that bad and not that often. He had been in a pretty good mood tonight considering she practically threw him out of the bar. Drinking did that to him though. Whenever he had hit her, he was always stone cold sober. Drinking just mellowed him out. Whenever she was around him, she kept him in booze.

Wanda walked back to the bar and wiped it down again. It had been two hours since the guy had left, and Wanda knew the sun would be up in another hour. That's all she needed. She could hear it now. Mrs. Blanchard would hear from that bitch, Angie, all about how she left the bar at five a.m.

"I'm outahere," she told herself and threw the washcloth into the sink. She walked to the door and looked over at the Post Office. She didn't see anyone, but raised her middle finger in that direction anyway. She felt a little better, but not much. Wanda locked the door and left.

Angie worked the night shift at the Post Office. She was five and a half feet tall with shoulder length, chestnut hair. Her blue and white postal uniform did nothing for her slender body. Her breasts were small but firm, some even referring to them as perky. With what little mail that did come into town, Angie could finish sorting it well before her shift ended. As a result, she spent most of the night flirting with the nightshift deputy whose office was right in back. They shared an alley and she frequently met with him early in the A.M.

Angie didn't see Wanda leave, though. In fact, she wouldn't have cared if she did. Angie was out behind the Post Office waiting for Phil Hartman. Phil was a deputy sheriff of five years and every bit the part. He was over six feet tall and weighed two hundred and twenty-five pounds. His strong, powerful torso cut an imposing portrait of the lawman. Despite his appearance, Phil was a quiet, some would say shy, man. He was also fairly drunk. He had spent most of the evening over at Sandy's when he should have been at home sleeping.

Angie, on the other hand, had finished early and was leaning against a dumpster, stoned on pot, when Phil came out of the Sheriff station.

"There's my baby," she said, looking at him with slits for eyes. "I was beginning to worry about you."

"Are you high again?" Phil asked with a noticeable distaste in his voice.

"Why, do you want some?"

"Angie, you know I can't: it against the law."

"What about you? You're drunk and you're supposed to be on duty."

"Maybe, but at least alcohol's legal."

"You're a hypocrite. The only reason why pot's illegal is because the gov'ment can't tax it. Ain't that so?"

"It has nothing to do with that. Mary Juwana is bad for you. It can make you sterile."

"Yeah, right, like you give a damn. Besides, what about last week? You were so drunk that you couldn't even get it up. Or at least that's what you said. I bet you were screwing that whore, Wanda. You seem to spend a lot of time over there lately."

"Angie! Dammit girl. It happens to be the only bar in town. Besides, she's hooked up with Kevin." Phil totally ignored the impotent remark. He didn't know why, but lately he was having problems, serious problems. It was one of the reasons he had been drinking like a fish. Some nights he was the only reason the doors were open at the bar.

"Why should that stop her?" Angie continued. "It wouldn't me. Come to think of it, I wouldn't mind having Kevin right now. I saw him leaving earlier tonight in a huff. Wanda wasn't with him. I bet he is all horned up and ready to go."

"Angie, shut your trap. I ain't playin'. Keep it up and I'm gonna..."

"You're gonna what, hit me? Go ahead. You know what I like." She said that sarcastically but it was true. She did like it rough. Truth of the matter, the remark she made concerning Phil's sexual prowess was more out of emotional hurt than anything else. She didn't really care if he was giving it to Wanda or not. What mattered was that he wasn't giving it to her.

The two of them had been meeting like this for over a year. Once a week, wham, bam, and oh! By the way, thank you! But lately, he couldn't or wouldn't get it up. She had tried—oh god she had tried—but nothing seemed to work. He acted like he just didn't want to touch her. Last time was the worst. She had stripped off all her clothes and was laying on a cot in the jail waiting for him. He just looked at her and then turned away. "Put your clothes back on," he had told her. She felt totally rejected.

"You want me to slap you around? Maybe I will," he said, moving around to grab her with both hands.

She tensed up but relaxed when he pulled her close and planted a long, hard, wet kiss on her lips. She returned the kiss just as passionately. Her hand reached down to the crotch of his pants and began to massage the slight bulge there. He didn't seem to mind and shuffled his feet outward a bit to make things a little more accommodating.

"Phil," she whispered. "I want you. I want you so bad." She quickly dropped to her knees and fumbled with his zipper.

"Not here," he breathed. "Inside." He took her hand and pulled her to her feet.

They half sprinted, half slid into the open back door of the police station. Once inside, Phil proceeded to rip open her shirt. Buttons flew off the white and blue postal shirt to reveal two firm, white breasts with nothing supporting them. She had already unzipped his starched, blue slacks and was reaching into the opening of his boxer shorts. He jerked her hand away and in one smooth, continuous move lifted her off the floor and into his arms. His slacks had fallen down around his feet and he managed to step out of them without falling over. The door to one of the cells was open and he carried her into it, laying her gently on the cot.

"What are you gonna do now, big boy?" she said, smiling up at him.

"What I should've done last week. C'mer!" Towering over her from one end of the cot, Phil reached down, grabbed her ankles in his dry, rough hands and lifted her legs up so that they were pointing straight in the air. He rested both of her legs on his broad shoulders and slowly knelt to the floor. Phil hadn't been this excited for a long time. He methodically loosened the belt and clasp of her slacks. The zipper parted effortlessly as he tugged gently on her belt loops, trying to get the slacks over her hips. She wiggled around trying to help. He stood up again and grabbed a hold of her pants legs, jerking them off. She was totally naked, except for her ripped-open blouse. Her shoes had been lost somewhere by the door.

Phil grinned down at her. He took off his shoes and kicked them out of the way. Defiantly, with jerky movements, he unbuttoned his shirt and took it off. Angie sat up and reached out for his shorts.

"Not yet," he said. "I'll be right back." He walked out of the cell and over to a desk in the middle of the room. Opening a drawer, he reached in and fumbled around looking for something, smiling when he found it. "Just in case you try to get away," he said, holding a pair of handcuffs.

Angie smiled dreamily at him. She was coming down from her High and felt very relaxed, ready to do whatever he wanted. She lay back down and threw her hands over her head.

"Uh-uh," he said. "Turn over. I've got different plans for you."

Willingly, she rolled over.

"Here," throwing the handcuffs at her. "Lie on your stomach and stick your hands between the head board railings. Now put those on."

She did, writhing with excitement. "Hurry, babeeey! I want you so bad."

Phil walked up behind her and pulled his shorts down, staring at his limp member. Nothing... Not one, damned thing. "Umrph," he mumbled.

"What's that baby?" she purred.

"Nothing," he said and slapped her on the ass. "Damn it to hell." He placed his hands on her butt cheeks and shoved. "What's the use?"

Angie hit her head against the railing and screamed. The impact left a cut on her head above her left eye; blood trickled from the wound down her face. "You son-of-a-bitch! What the hell did you do that for? Phil?"

Phil left the cell and headed to the back door. He stopped there and picked up his pants. He glanced over at the cell, seeing the compromising position Angie was in cuffed to the cot. He shrugged and put on his pants. "I'll be back in a minute."

"Leaving? Where you going? Come back here you son-of-a-bitch. Don't leave me here like this. What if somebody comes in?"

"He can have you," he said slamming the door.

Phil had reached a breaking point. He knew he had a problem and the drinking wasn't helping matters any. Instead of thinking of what he should do to correct the problem, he directed all of his frustration and anger at Angie. It was her, he thought. She was the cause of his impotency. She was probably in there laughing at him, humping the pillow. "That bitch," he said aloud. He calmly reached for the cigarettes that should have been in his shirt pocket and grabbed a nipple instead. "Damn!"

Phil looked at the back door. He could hear her screaming for him. He walked over to it and reached for the knob. He stopped. *The hell with her,* he thought. *Let her whine if she wants. The next shift won't be here until eight. I have plenty of time. She's gonna hate me for leaving her cuffed to the bed, but so what? What's that compared to this?*

He looked down at himself with a grimace. The big, virile Phil Hartman was nothing more than a gelding. He couldn't get it up with a tow truck. He hated Angie for that. It was all her fault. At one time he had thought he loved her. But now, he hated her. He began to think of her in terms he would apply to a streetwalker. The hostility towards her was building. It fed on his insecurities and burned within him. Then he heard a voice. Quiet at first, but then it grew louder. The more pain and humiliation he felt, the louder the voice became.

"Kill her," the voice said. "Kill her and all your troubles will be over."

Phil listened to that voice, appalled, but considering. The blackness that had entered him began to grow. It took his pain and turned it into hate. The hate boiled and consumed him from within. His face took on a twisted appearance and he knew the truth. Ever since high-school he had a problem with his sexual organ. He remembered making up excuses to the girls he dated. Some of them figured out the truth and laughed at him.

"She's laughing at you now," the voice mocked.

Phil remembered one girl he had failed with. "What's the matter," she had said, "Like boys or something?" That girl went around telling everyone about it. Even now, he could hear them chanting, "Philly is silly. He plays with boys willies."

"Are you silly, Philly?" the voice said.

Phil drove his trembling fingers into his hair. "Leave me alone," he screamed.

"Angie looks just like that girl from school, doesn't she Philly? In fact, they all do. Every last one of them. Can't you hear them? Listen! They're calling your queer, Phil. And as long as you can't get it up, they might as well be right, right?"

"No! I'm not a queer." Arguing with no one, Phil had stepped over that imaginary line between sanity and insanity.

"If you're not, then prove it. She's in there all tied up. Show her who the boss is. C'mon. You've got the balls, don't ya?"

"Yeah, I've got the balls and a whole lot more. I'll make her bark like a dog." Phil began to laugh, chuckling to the emptiness of the lot.

19

The bell on the front door rang and Angie looked up. She was still lying on her stomach with her arms stretched out over her head. She tried to prop herself up on her elbows to get a look at who was coming in. It was getting light outside and she hoped it was Phil. The next shift came in at eight, but that didn't mean anything. She was naked and handcuffed to a cot and felt very vulnerable. The last thing she wanted was to be found this way. She would never forgive Phil for this.

The figure that came through the door definitely wasn't Phil. The cell was partially hidden behind a three-foot partition and she lifted herself up enough to see above it. When she did all she could see was the back of a man's head as he turned and closed the door. His hair was long and blonde and fell across his shoulders. She quickly lay back down. She decided she did not know this man but didn't know if that was good or bad. *If I lie still,* she thought, *maybe he won't see me and go away. After all, Phil has to come back sometime and let me loose.*

"Hello? Is anybody home?" the man said. "Come now, I know you're in here, I can smell you."

Smell me? Angie tensed. She instinctively lowered her head beneath her arms hoping, somehow, he wouldn't see her.

The footsteps came closer, each step echoing in the quiet building. Angie heard them loud and clear, noticing they weren't shuffling around like a man searching for something but took a slow, leisurely pace in her direction. She chanced a peek out of the corner of her eye and saw the top of his head growing with every step.

Angie wiggled around a bit making sure nothing of her front showed. She crossed her legs and arched her head back, forcing it above her shoulders. When his eyes appeared above the wooden partition she locked onto them. He was smiling, she wasn't.

"L-L-Look, I know what this must look like but there is a really good explanation for this." Angie was more than nervous; she was terrified.

"Lady, it doesn't matter what the explanation is because I'm enjoying this immensely."

"I'm s-s-sure you are, but I need to get out of here."

"And I suppose you want me to let you loose. Do you take me for the fool? Whatever the Sheriff does with his prisoners is none of my business."

"I'm not a prisoner. Look. The cell door is open."

"You're right, good point."

"So could you let me out of here? My clothes are on the floor."

"What would you have me do? I think I'll try and find the Sheriff."

"NO! I mean he's not here." Angie tried to think quickly. "He split for awhile and left me like this. I guess he didn't realize how early it was. I mean, normally people don't come in here this early."

"And how is it that you would know? Have you and the Sheriff done this sort of thing before? Or is it the Deputy you like?"

Angie thought for a moment. What did she care what this guy thought? He didn't live around here, and even if he did manage to tell a few people, most of them would give Phil a "high five". "Okay, look. Yeah. We have a thing going and we lost track of time. All I need is the key to the cuffs and I'm out of here."

"And where might that be?"

"They're hanging there on the wall, on his belt, the little key." Angie had lost most of her fear and her anger was returning.

The man reached for the key and then stopped. Attached to the belt was a baton and he grabbed that instead.

"Why did you get that?" Angie asked, panic coming back into her eyes.

"For all I know, you may be lying. I don't want to take any chances."

"Look, don't have a cow. Do you think I could really hurt you?"

"Maybe not, but maybe I want to hurt you."

"What?" Angie said in shocked disbelief.

Beliah walked over to the cell door, pounding the baton into the palm of his hand with every step. "The only reason why a woman would let herself be tied up like that is if she was a naughty girl."

She knew what he meant. This man was a sicko' and he was going to hurt her, bad. "Leave me alone!" She twitched and twisted against the cuffs, cutting her wrists.

"Now, now my good woman. No need for that. If I want you to scream, I would give you reason to." With that he moved in and whacked her butt with the baton.

"Aaahhhh!" she screamed.

"Oh, that didn't hurt now, did it?" Beliah chuckled to himself. He raised the baton again and brought it down on the small of her back, crushing vertebrae.

"Uhhn!" Angie let out a whimper. The pain was excruciating and she was on the verge of passing out. In the back of her mind she knew the pain wouldn't last much longer because by the looks of things she was going to die.

"Is that the best you can do? Come, now. I want to really hear some noise." He raised the baton once again and brought it down on her butt.

She screamed again. "Please! Stop!" Tears were streaming down her face. Her left butt cheek was split wide open and blood trickled across and down her hip.

"You're begging now? And I thought you were such a vain woman, too." Beliah raised the baton again and brought it down hard, cracking her in the head. Her head split open like a cantaloupe. He raised and lowered the baton again and again, beating her to a pulp. The mattress soaked up the blood like a sponge and he kept swinging that baton until Angie was quite dead.

20

Phil heard the screams but was unable to move. Something was holding him back. A psychologist would have said his immobility was due to his unconscious desire to have Angie experience pain. That might be so, but he was a seasoned professional. When someone screamed like that it meant they were in serious trouble and he was trained to respond.

Phil fought with himself for several minutes before finally moving. Whatever kept him from moving released him in such a way that the force of his own will drove him to the ground. Without noticing the sharp pain and small cut on his right knee, he got to his feet and ran the short distance to the door.

Phil tore the door opened and saw that everything was how he had left it—except for one major difference. He stood, mouth agape, staring at the scene before him. The cell door was opened and there was blood everywhere. The floor was covered in dark crimson from the cot to the bars, spreading out into the office. Seeing Angie lying limp and lifeless, Phil rushed over to her and slipped in the bloody goo, falling onto the cot and on top of Angie.

"Angie?" She didn't move. He skated past the cell door and bolted to the front of the building. It was well after dawn and the sun cast a golden beam of light through a jar in the door. He flung the door open and ran outside. Madison Avenue was early-morning quiet.

Phil was desperate. Who could have done that? Without a suspect, the blame would fall on him, and rightly so. There was no way he could explain what happened in there. He went back in and said, "What am I gonna do? Craig's gonna be here in an hour."

Phil glanced over at the cell. He couldn't see her body at that angle but instead saw the blood running around the partition. "Get rid of her, that's what I'll do. Get rid of her."

21

Jason went outside and watched the sun come up. He sat in a plastic lawn chair, throwing a ball to his dog, sipping on lukewarm lemonade. Thoughts of the night before whirled through his head. The death of Mr. Richardson was bad enough, but to be plagued by those dreams made it even worse. He still hadn't come to terms with calling his dreams "OBE's". Although he felt out of body, the experiences were too unbelievable to be anything else but a dream. But they seem so real! Tonka ran up to Jason with a spit-covered ball wedged between his massive jaws and landed squarely in Jason's lap, almost knocking him over, bringing him back to reality.

"Good boy." He threw the ball as hard as he could to the back of his one acre yard. But before the ball could hit the ground the part boxer/part hound but all muscle mutt was under the ball waiting for it to land. With a chomp, Tonka swallowed the ball and rushed back to Jason.

He watched the dog sprint towards him and his speed excited him. With every step Tonka's muscles flexed showing the cuts in his shoulders and hindquarters. What a sight! Jason knew why people feared his dog, and at times he played with that fear. He wondered if the Dark Thing from his dreams would fear Tonka. He took two large swallows of his drink, finishing it off. "Ah!" he sighed. "There's nothing like a shot of sugar to get you going in the morning."

Tonka pounced on his lap again and Jason rubbed the dog's head energetically. "Good boy. Gooooood boy," he whispered.

"Woof! Woof! Woof!" Tonka barked in agreement.

"Tic, tic, tic. Go on boy, go play," Jason said, shooing his dog away. As much as he loved playing with his dog, he couldn't keep his mind away from last night. He thought of Tommy, his best friend—next to Tonka, of course—and wondered how he was holding up.

Jason still couldn't believe Tommy's father killed himself. He knew Mr. Richardson and he didn't seem like the kind of fellow to do that sort of thing. Mr. Richardson always had a joke and a pat on the back for Jason. He knew that their business had fallen off lately, but Tommy said that it had something to do with a guy named Brady in Washington, DC. Jason had asked Mr. Langley over at the garage if he knew anything about it, considering he was from DC, and he had said that Brady was the guy who got shot protecting Ronald Reagan a few years back. Jason remembered something like that happening, but didn't see the connection. Still, that was no reason for him to kill himself.

Jason stood up and stretched. The sun was warm and his stomach told him he was hungry. He wondered if Tommy still wanted to grab a bite to eat at the cafe and then go over to the bookstore. That was the plan two days ago, but now how should he act? Tonka sat down at his feet and whined. Jason looked at him and smiled, patting the dog's head. "You're right boy. I'll give him a call and walk on over there."

The dog tried wiggling the short nub he had for a tail but only accomplished moving his rear end around. Jason thought if he was hurting, as he knew Tommy must be hurting, that he would want to be with his best friend. Tonka barked, seeming to read his mind, and Jason said, "You know I mean you, but Tommy doesn't have a dog. I'm all he has." Jason thought for a second and then added, "Now."

Jason opened the sliding glass door and went inside. The house was quiet and somewhat dark, adding to the fact that his parents were obviously still asleep. He thought about waking them, but decided against it. He reached for the cordless phone and punched the seven digits of Tommy's number. After the first ring, the answering machine picked up with Mr. Richardson's voice asking the caller to please leave a message. Jason was horrified at the ghastly narration on the other end. He dropped the phone, but quickly picked it up. Apparently, someone at the house had turned the machine on to accept the calls of any sympathetic neighbor without thinking about the voice on the tape.

Jason knew he had to get over there soon before the whole town heard the voice of a dead man. He scratched out a note and left it by the coffee pot for his parents to see and hurried out the back door, almost tripping over Tonka as he went.

Tommy's house was off of Lee Street, like Jason's house, but one block over. A creek lined with a thick growth of pecan trees separated the two blocks from each other and Jason headed in that direction. The two of them had gone this way to each other's house since they were kids, wearing a permanent path to follow. He was almost to the creek when he heard a sound right on his heels. It was Tonka.

"Dog!" Jason stopped walking and looked back over his shoulder. Shrugging, he said, "Okay, come on. I'm sure he'll be glad to see you, too."

Together, they sprinted towards the creek and Jason tried to jump the width of it. He came down hard just short of the far bank and twisted his ankle slightly. Tonka managed to clear the creek with room to spare and continued down the path a short ways until he noticed Jason wasn't behind him. He sat down panting, waiting for Jason to catch up. Jason picked himself up and started running, grimacing a little in response to the prickly sensation he felt in his ankle.

They broke through the trees and Jason saw Tommy's house a few yards away. When he reached the back fence surrounding the house he stopped and bent over to catch his breath. Tonka barked as a shadowy figure came to the darkened, draped back door and looked out. Jason straightened up and looked at the figure. It was Tommy.

Tommy appeared to Jason exactly how a boy would look if he had just lost his father. He had dark circles under his eyes caused by either a lack of sleep or hours spent crying, probably both. His shoulders were slumped and his head hung low. He opened the sliding glass door and forced a smile.

"Hey, Jason," he sighed.

"Hey, Tommy. How... how are you?"

"I'm makin' it okay. I'm glad you came over. I was wonderin' if you would."

"Whatdya mean? Of course I was gonna come over. We were gonna go see that writer fellow, I mean if you want to. I'd understand if you don't."

"Yeah. Come on in. My mom's still at the hospital. She's not taking it too well."

"Stay, Tonka."

Tommy pulled the curtain back and Jason stepped into a room that looked more like a morgue. They were in the basement of a two-story house with the only source of natural light being the glass door. With that covered by thick, dark-brown drapes and no lights on it was pitch-black.

"Kinda dark, isn't it Tommy?"

"I guess. I don't much care to see anything or be seen."

Jason let that remark go without any comment. Tommy, he thought, must really be hurting. They sat down in two recliners, Tommy with a plop and Jason after almost tripping over it. "You said your mother's at the hospital?"

"Yeah. They got her doped-up on Valium or somethin'. Sheriff Dunn said she was in shock, probably because she saw what dad looked like."

Jason's stomach growled and that reminded him of one of the reasons he came over to Tommy's in the first place. Then he remembered the phone. He got up and walked over to the answering machine and flicked it off. Tommy didn't say anything and Jason wondered if Tommy knew exactly why he did it.

"You ah... hungry?" Jason asked.

"I don't know. Maybe. You?"

As if in response to the question, his stomach gurgled again.

"I guess you are. There's stuff in the refrigerator. Help yourself." Tommy paused for a moment and then said, "Or did you want to eat at the cafe like we planned?"

"I kinda did. I was looking forward to hearing what all the older people thought of the meeting last night. The place should be crowded."

"That's the problem."

"What do you mean?" The words were barely out of Jason's mouth when he realized what Tommy meant. The comment made a few minutes earlier came back to him. Tommy had said he didn't care too much to see or be seen. Jason felt like a jerk. The meeting, although explosive, wouldn't be on the town's mind as much as Tommy's father. The writer was unusual, yes, but the accident was something altogether different.

"Well, I..."

"Tommy, I'm sorry. I wasn't thinkin'. If you don't want to go that's fine with me. We don't have to go see that Beliah guy either."

"But you were looking forward to it. You wanted to ask him about those dreams you've been having. Hey, what about that? Anything?"

"We don't need to talk about my nightmares. Yours are a lot worse, they're real."

"It would be good for me to talk about something else. At least I know I'm not the only one losing their mind." Tommy gave Jason a half smile, one with a hint of sarcastic humor.

"Screw you!"

They both laughed at that and it felt really good. Jason noticed an immediate change in Tommy's manner and decided he liked it. It felt good to see his friend laughing and a good hardy laugh at that. He knew things were going to be okay for Tommy. Tommy was a strong kid and that was the main reason why Jason hung around him, although he hadn't a clue as to why Tommy hung out with him. But that really didn't matter. What did matter was that his friend was still in one piece.

"So what about it? Have any lately?"

While Tommy appeared more relaxed, Jason became increasingly uneasy. Those dreams bothered him. Tommy was right. He did want to talk to Beliah about them. From what he had learned the book dealt with magic and the special powers that all people had but just didn't know about. Jason hoped that maybe it dealt with his special power. He desperately wanted to talk to Beliah, now more than ever.

"Yeah I have, and they're getting worse. I had one last night that was just terrible."

"Last night?"

"Yeah. I've had them for the past two nights. I couldn't get back to sleep after the one last night."

"Well, what are they about?"

"They're not about anything, really. It's just me in my house with a woman."

Tommy smiled at that. "Yeah, I know that kind. I have them myself. I've had to change the sheets before—"

"I'm not talkin' about wet dreams, you moron." That came out wrong and Jason wished he hadn't called him that, but he was on the verge of cracking up. "I'm talking about being followed by a dark force that eats your soul and then you're dead. The woman's more like a guide, but the dark thing is evil. He's there every night now. Tommy, I'm afraid to go to sleep any more." Jason started crying and couldn't stop. "I'm scared. He's gonna get me, I know it."

"I didn't know. I'm sorry. I didn't mean to make a joke of it. Why didn't you tell me earlier it was getting this bad? Maybe I could've helped."

Jason, now in control of himself said, "Look at me. You lost your father last night and I'm the one ballin' like a baby. I'm the one who should be sorry, not you. I shouldn't have jumped on you like that. I'm sorry."

Jason snorted and wiped the tears out of his eyes. He felt a thousand times better. Sharing his secret with Tommy allowed a sense of relief to cover him. It didn't seem as bad now as it did early this morning. He was glad he had a friend like Tommy to talk to.

"I guess I'm not much help to you, am I?" Jason said, slightly embarrassed.

"Actually you are. By listening and watching you it sort of puts my life in perspective. I mean, I love my dad and all, and I will miss him, sure. But ever since he started his own business I haven't really seen him. He was always gone. I've grown up without him for so long that I don't know how to miss him now that he's gone for good. That's why I needed to see him last night as he was. It made it real to me. I was feeling bad because I didn't feel bad. I mean, I feel for my mom and I know it's gonna be tough, but I think we can make it." Tommy let that set in for a moment and then said, "Is it wrong not to feel bad?"

"I don't know, Tommy. I...," and then he didn't have anything else to say.

"Well," Tommy said after a few minutes of silence. "I don't know about you but I'm starved."

"Yeah, me too." Jason was pleased the conversation picked up again. He started to feel funny and Tommy looked like he was about to slide back into his mood. He was hungry and glad that Tommy was too.

"Then let's get out of here. You gonna take Tonka?"

"Sure, why not?"

"I just hope Earl doesn't see him. I swear that last time he almost hit him."

"Screw him. If he gets anywhere near my dog, I'll shoot him." Jason grimaced at that. It was strange being around someone whose father had shot himself, whether on purpose or not. He was afraid of saying anything that might upset his friend. He looked at Tommy, who didn't seem to even have heard the remark, but felt bad just the same.

They made it outside and Jason whistled for Tonka. The dog was over in the neighbors' yard marking his territory, and after finishing his business, bounced over to them. The boys walked down the middle of the road while the dog zigzagged between them. A quarter of a mile later the road intersected Lee Street and they took a left. Less than a mile later they came to Main Street and turned the corner. Just in front of them to the left was the gun store. They continued walking, but Jason guessed at what Tommy must be thinking.

Jason didn't know why they came this way. Usually they would have cut across Lee Street and hiked through the woods. Damn, he thought. Everything he said or did seemed to come right back at him. He knew that Tommy could have just as easily gone the other way, but Jason scolded himself for not thinking ahead. He began thinking about the cafe and what they must be talking about right this minute. He sneaked a sideways glance at Tommy to see how he was taking it. Tommy appeared unmoved. After what he had said to Jason concerning his father, Jason wondered if Tommy had in fact gotten over the death so soon. He doubted it, but he didn't know.

"Did you see Missy last night at the meeting?" Tommy asked.

"Missy? Yeah, she was up front. I figured you two were fighting or something so I didn't bring it up. Were you?"

"I don't know. I was supposed to meet her at the soda shop around three. I was running late and couldn't get there until four. She wasn't there. I guess she got mad and left. What a bitch."

"Women."

"What do you know about it," Tommy said, laughing.

"Lot more than you, I see."

"Jason, you haven't had a woman since a woman had you."

"Watch it, redneck. That's my mamma you're talking about. Tonka, get 'em boy."

"Like right, I'm scared. He doesn't have a mean bone in his body. C'mer boy." Tommy stopped and patted his chest with one hand. Tonka placed his front paws on top of Tommy's shoulders and licked him hard, covering his face in rancid dog breath and spittle.

"Maybe, but he'll lick you to death." They both laughed and Jason felt good again. This was the same old friend he had grown up with, wise cracks and all. It was good to see Tommy and Tonka playing like that. If anything were different about Tommy, Tonka would have known it.

"Come on," Tommy said, pushing the dog back. He raced away from him, and once Tonka regained his balance, chased after him. "I'll beat you to the cafe, virgin."

"Not if I get there first, you panty-waste."

They sprinted to the cafe not even pausing at the intersection with Commerce. Tonka stayed between the two of them not sure if he was pursuing or being pursued. Jason made it to the cafe first and flung the door open.

"See," Tommy said, trying to catch his breath. "Virgins have more energy. Sex saps your strength."

"Should I ask Missy about that?"

Tommy's cheeks redden. They both knew Tommy hadn't scored with Missy yet, but that wasn't news. Missy didn't give it up and that was no secret.

They walked in and Jason was relieved to find the place relatively empty with only a few people scattered here and there. Must have been a late night for everyone, he thought. Tonka sat outside and pressed his nose against the glass door, looking in with sincere anticipation.

"Don't worry boy, I'll bring you somethin'. Hey, let's sit over there."

22

A bell rang and Phil Hartman jumped out of his chair. He felt sure it was the bell hanging on the door signaling the arrival of someone. After the second ring, though, he grabbed the phone. "Hello? Craig? Yeah, I'm fine, just... what? Uh, sure... sure... No problem at all. Take all the time you need, I could use the over-time. Take the whole day... What? Okay, I'll see you then. Get some sleep. Bye."

"Hot damn," he said. The phone call had been from his boss. Phil expected to see him anytime now standing at the front door staring at the ghoulish mess that still partially covered the jail floor. Instead, Craig called to ask him if he could stay a little longer. Sheriff Dunn had been up all night collecting information about the Richardson death and he wanted to get a couple hours sleep before he came in to relieve Phil.

Phil didn't have any problem with that whatsoever. Looking back at the mess he knew he wouldn't have had time to clean it up, much less get rid of the body. He thought of Angie and what had happened less than an hour ago and suddenly realized that Craig could have come in at any time throughout the night. Phil had completely forgotten about what had happened at the gun store. He remembered the phone call from Dunn shortly after he clocked on duty and the Sheriff wasn't too happy.

"Where the hell have you been," he had said. "I've been trying to find you for the last couple of hours. You weren't at home and nobody had seen you for most of the day."

He was pissed, Phil remembered. But how could he tell him he had been at Sandy's getting drunk right before his shift? All he could do was stumble over his words and hope he didn't sound drunk.

Craig had told him what happened and left it at that. It was only when he went out to see Angie and she got him so worked up that he'd forgotten Craig was roaming the streets. He felt ill. Part of him felt lucky while the other part reminded him of the bloody corpse slowly stinking up the cell.

It didn't matter, he thought. He had more important things to contend with right now, namely: how to get the body out without being seen in the ever-increasing daylight; and more importantly, where to take it. He couldn't load it up, drive somewhere out of town while leaving the jail looking like a scene from a cheap horror movie. But to wait until after he cleaned the place up would increase his chances of being caught. He didn't like this one bit. He found himself getting deeper and deeper into something that really wasn't his fault. He thought again about just calling Dunn and telling him what was up, but that would mean losing his job, his wife, the respect of the town and Angie all in one swipe. He would have to leave town and everything he knew and start all over with nothing.

He closed his eyes and shook his head, trying to clear it. No, he told himself. He had already lied to Dunn by not telling him the truth and his options were limited. His first priority would be to get Angie's body out of the cell and into the trunk of the cruiser. The blood he might be able to explain away, but a body, never.

He carefully made his way over to the cell and grabbed a blanket off of a shelf before entering. The handcuffs were still on Angie's wrists and he could see the marks there where she had struggled, in vain, trying to get away from her attacker. He started sobbing with the realization that even though he wasn't the one who killed her he was the one that placed her in a position for this to happen.

Still sobbing, he placed the gray, woolen blanket on the floor by the cot and rolled her bloody body onto it. He couldn't bare the thought of lifting her enough to get the blanket around her while looking into her face, so he knelt down without touching the floor with his knees and draped the blanket over her. It reminded him of a burrito (a meaty one with lots of chunky salsa, his mind called back to him). Phil fought down the urge to vomit and lifted the body over his broad shoulders.

He started for the front door and then thought better of it. He made a U-turn and headed for the back and the alley, managing to open the door with one hand while balancing the body with the other. He scanned the alley, making sure it was clear, and dropped his load hard on the pavement.

Sweating now, due mostly to nerves than anything else, he hurried around to the side of the building and his car parked there. He popped the trunk and ran back to get the bundle. A cat was sniffing at one of the openings and again he felt sick, although this time he couldn't hold it back. His stomach turned and the vomit came in a muddy flood of foul-smelling liquid.

Beer was the only thing he had put in his stomach since yesterday afternoon, but that ceased flowing almost immediately followed by bright-yellow bile. He dry heaved for what seemed like ten minutes before he could stop. His sides were killing him and he felt like dying. The cat ran over to his mess and started licking it up. He was about to have another episode when he forced himself away and back to the job at hand. He couldn't decide which was worse: the cat drinking his puke, or the blood-soaked blanket attracting the interest of other alley creatures. Either option made him nauseous.

He loaded the bloody bundle up and closed the trunk. Grabbing a mop and bucket from the water closet by the back door, Phil filled the bucket with cold water and large amounts of bleach and made his way back inside. The room had the smell of a slaughterhouse and Phil felt, for the first time, the full impact of what had happened: This was murder and he was an accessory after the fact. He felt his world collapsing around him. With Angie in his trunk, he knew he would be spending time in prison. If not for life, then at least for the next twenty years. He had no choice but to cover up, completely, no loose ends and definitely no remorse.

He scrubbed and mopped the floor to a shine using several buckets of water and several rolls of paper towels. He put the mattress and paper towels out back in the dumpster. He grabbed a gas can he had in the shed out back and poured about a gallon of gas on the mattress. He threw in a lighted match and ignited the blood-soaked mattress, hoping nobody would see the smoke rising from the dumpster. After letting it burn for a few minutes he threw a bucket of water on it, causing it to smoke even more. Explaining a burnt mattress would be easy, he thought, but not a bloody one.

He went back inside and sprayed the air with deodorant. He knew he would have to come up with a story for the mattress, but overall he was quite please with himself. It was going on nine o'clock and Phil was ecstatic.

He sat at the desk with his feet propped up and said, "Anytime you're ready, Sheriff."

23

Sheriff Craig Dunn opened the door to the jailhouse exactly at ten and caught Phil napping at his desk. "Hasn't been too busy, has it?"

"Whaa?" Phil's first thought was that of Angie and he momentarily panicked, spilling his large feet off of the desk and onto the floor with a thud. "Craig, I didn't hear you come in."

"That much is obvious. Any excitement last night?"

"Well, yes. I was invaded by a bunch of crabs. They were overrunnin' the place."

"Crabs? Phil, what are you talkin' about?"

"On the mattress, in the cell. It was crawling with crabs. I guess that guy we had in here last week brought them in. I had to burn it. It's in the dumpster out back." Phil thought for a moment and then said, "I did it this morning."

"Uh, huh. Look, this Richardson thing has got me bothered. Something's not right."

"It's never right when it happens to someone you know."

"Yeah, but I'm not talkin' about that. I don't think it was an accident or a suicide. Things just don't add up."

"So tell me what you've got."

Craig spent the next twenty minutes relaying the events of the past twelve hours up to and including the grizzly scene at the gun store. "But I have no motive and no suspect."

"Do you need me to stay and help you dig up clues?"

"No, no. You go home and get some sleep. I'm not too sure what I'd have you do even if you were here. By the way, where were you last night? I called you every ten minutes on the radio and at home, but nothing. I couldn't even get Cathy."

"I, ah... Cathy!" He hit the palm of his hand on his forehead and the gesture reminded Dunn of a "V8" commercial. "You just reminded me. I plain forgot with staying late and then you telling me about Richardson. I have to get home. It has to do with Cathy and why you couldn't get me. I don't have the time to tell you. Cathy's gonna skin me alive. I gotta go."

He bolted for the door and said over his shoulder, "I'll explain everything later. See ya, Craig." And then he was gone.

Phil knew it was a lame excuse and he knew Craig would think it was a lame excuse. It sounded like a man trying to cover up something, which he was, but he hoped Craig was too immersed in Richardson to think twice about not being able to get in touch with him. He got into his cruiser and pulled away. Five miles out of town he approached a stop sign and proceeded across the intersection towards Cooter's pond.

"You did very good," a voice inside him said. "You're free and clear now. After you dump the bitch in the drink, we go after your wife."

My wife? Phil wondered.

"Yes. The bitch wasn't home when she should've been. She's supposed to cover for you when you're out drinking, but the asshole Sheriff said he couldn't get her to answer the phone. Where was she, Phil? Where was she?"

The question repeated itself in his mind, quickly working on his sanity, pushing him to think of his wife in terms he never thought of her before. Phil really did love his wife, though maybe not like a husband should. But she was always there for him, even when she caught him with Angie that time in their bed. She was hurt, yes, but she never left him or told a soul. Phil loved and respected her for that and even tried to change. Phil stayed away from Angie and went as far as to tell Craig about the affair so he could help him avoid Angie.

That worked for a while until the night she came to the jail with handcuffs. It began again, but it was different somehow. It was more sex than anything else. There was no commitment, which was why Phil started to have problems getting it up. He realized he was betraying the only woman he ever truly loved for a cheap slut with overactive hormones and an S&M fetish. And that, he thought, was the beginning of the end. A tear rolled down his face and he knew that no matter what happened now it would never be the same.

"But she wasn't there, Phil. I bet she was screwing Jim Langley. She always did like him, didn't she Phil? Isn't it odd to you that her car broke down so much last year? I bet that is where it started. That bitch. I bet she's with him right now, laughing at you. I bet the whole town knows. I bet that's what sheriff Dunny wunny was trying to tell you. Look Phil, ole buddy ole pal, you've already got rid of one problem, why not take care of that other one? She's bound to tell Dunn about your drinking. Do it now before it's too late. Do it now!"

Phil snapped. The weight of his actions had found a small hole in his conscience and worked its way through to the core of his being. He started laughing hysterically, stomping the accelerator to the floor. The digital speedometer read 95 when he missed the turn and veered off the road. He hit an embankment and the car flew through the air into a tree. It landed tail end down and flipped over on the roof, popping the trunk open and spilling Angie's body out and away from the car. In the silence that only the woods can produce all that could be heard was the low erratic moan of a man barely alive.

24

Pastor Blanchard looked at his watch and then put his bible down. He was physically exhausted. After spending half the night with Mrs. Richardson at the hospital, and then coming home to find it taken over by Doris and her lady friends, he felt like he needed a long vacation. Sleeping was a nightmare. He woke up every hour or so believing he was being chased by a dark man. The name of that writer, Beliah, showed up in his dreams flashing across his awareness like a theater marquee. He couldn't figure it out.

Now, however, it was morning and getting late. He needed to run down to the hospital and check on Mrs. Richardson and her son, if he could find him. His call earlier this morning to the Richardson's went unanswered. Tommy didn't or wouldn't or—and he feared this the most—couldn't answer. He looked at his watch again and decided to drive over to see Tommy, if he was there, and then head out for the hospital.

He climbed out of his recliner and took his coffee cup into the kitchen. Doris had her head stuck in the frig looking for something. He said: "I think I'm going to see Mrs. Richardson for awhile. You need anything while I'm out?"

"Mmmhf mhfft."

"What? Doris, I can't understand a thing you say with your mouth full."

Gulp! "I said, I don't think so. I think I'm going over to see Hillary."

"Don't you two ever get tired of talking about people?"

"Not when there's so much happening around here. Did you know that Wanda Pritchard didn't leave work until five o'clock this morning and Kevin wasn't with her?"

"Now what's that suppose to mean. If he had been with her you would have said something about that. How do you know, anyway?" Blanchard realized he must be stressed to take on his wife twice in twenty-four hours.

"Well, Hillary told me that Vicky told her that—"

"Wait, I don't want to know. I'm sorry I asked. I'll see you later... sweetheart." That last he had to force out.

Blanchard got in his Buick and backed down the gravel driveway. A few years back he would have walked to work just to enjoy the weather. But lately the walk seemed to get harder and harder. He knew the distance hadn't changed, so he concluded that it must be him getting older, not so much physically as mentally. Living with a wife like Doris would run any man down, he kidded himself, but he thanked God everyday for the chance to make things better. And today, he prayed, would be better than yesterday.

CHAPTER 5

Thought and emotion create reality.
From The Book of Beliah
Verse 30

25

WANDA QUIETLY OPENED THE DOOR of her trailer so as not to wake Kevin. She tip-toed into the small, two-room trailer and laid her purse on the beer can cluttered, round kitchen table. She adjusted the blinds over the kitchen sink and the first rays of dawn filtered into the room, casting a dull light on her overflowing trashcan. The stench was horrible.

She opened the refrigerator and found it devoid of anything edible. There was a moldy-looking, fuzz-covered growth left over from days (or was it weeks?) before that had been a poor attempt at meatloaf. She reached for the lone milk carton on the top shelf and set it down on the table.

"Uhumm." The noise came from the bedroom to her left and she crossed the room less cautiously now knowing full well that Kevin would be out cold until noon.

Wanda felt a little guilty and agitated with herself over what had happened earlier. The guilt came from blowing off her man like she did for a complete stranger and the agitation from not going home with him. She chuckled to herself, shaking her head. She couldn't remember the last time someone had turned her on to that extent, if there ever had been a time.

She didn't quite know why, but now that she was home with her man sleeping soundly in the next room, she was glad the stranger didn't come back. Screwing every guy that caught her eye just wasn't her thing anymore. A couple years ago yes, but not now. Now, she was a one-man woman, even though most of them didn't last very long.

She heard Kevin mumbling again and smiled brightly, happy in the knowledge that this one had lasted two years. Oh sure, he slept over half of the time, but there was a difference between sharing a bed with someone and sharing a home with them. Whatever the reason, it seemed to work for them and she really did love him, although not the way a wife would. This was more like a concerned friend kind of love; the only kind of love Wanda would ever let herself have with a male.

"You're nothing but a whore," her mind screamed at her, bringing a deep memory to the surface. In the dark recesses of her soul was the voice of a past too painful to relive. It was a hurt and betrayal of the most terrible kind.

"You're nothing but a whore," she heard the memory of her father say.

Whore, she thought. What did he know about it or even want to know about it. He didn't even believe her. It *did* happen. That much she had no doubt. But the disbelief and revulsion she had felt made the incident seem less important and more damaging in the long run.

"That just doesn't happen, now does it? If it did, you must have wanted it to happen. You seduced him into it. What with your slutty clothes and whorey make-up. You look just like your mom, and she's a whore. Is that what you are, a whore? You whore." He had screamed at her back then and now her mind repeated it with the same heartbreaking sting and shame.

Tears welled up in her eyes and she fought them back. *It did happen, she told herself, and you didn't do anything wrong. That priest seduced you and fondled your breasts while grabbing at your crotch. He placed his hand under your skirt and over your panties. You tried to stop him and he gave you some garbage about it was God's will for you to take care of his sexual needs. What a bunch of crap.* She was sobbing now and the hot tears felt good running down her cheek. They tasted salty and warm.

She usually never allowed herself this emotion, thinking it was weak, and weakness had put her at a disadvantage that one Sunday afternoon in the priest's office. She cried then, too. Never again, she had told herself.

Never again would she show weakness in front of a man and put herself at a disadvantage. She glowed with an intense desire to kill—not all men, just one: The one who had robbed her of her youth and innocence and left her with a shell of doubt and confusion, questioning her own identity.

She threw the milk carton across the room and it hit the wall, splattering sour milk and watching it slide down the wall. She thought briefly of cleaning it up before it stunk up the whole trailer, but decided that right then she didn't give a damn. She needed a drink, bad, but held back the urge. Alcoholism was one habit she had that she couldn't break, but had enough sense to keep a strong hand on it. She only drank with friends and when she was happy, which, for the latter, was very seldom now.

Wanda took an off-white towel out of a drawer by the sink and wiped up the mess, tossing it into the sink after she was finished. Kevin moaned for the third time and she grabbed a small bucket from under the sink and took it with her into the bedroom. She had no intentions of cleaning up his puke no matter how hung over he would be when he woke up. That, she thought, was something even a wife shouldn't have to do.

She quickly undressed and remembered only after taking off her jeans that she didn't have any panties on. She thought about taking a shower to get rid of the beer smell but decided against it, knowing with Kevin in his present state she would still smell like stale beer. She climbed into the small twin bed and curled up next to him, placing her head in the crook of his right arm. She leaned over and kissed him on the cheek, hoping that, yes, he would wake up and service her. After all that had happened tonight and the reliving of that brutal memory just a few minutes ago, she was as turned on as ever. *That's your problem*, she thought. *That's how you get into so much trouble. You let your body control your mind.* She mentally shrugged and rolled over on her back, frustrated, unable to wake Kevin from his self-induced coma.

Wanda watched a cockroach scurry across the ceiling and she fell into a dreamy trance filled with sexual imagery. Slowly, she worked one hand across her breast and then proceeded down past her tight stomach. She stopped short of her intended goal and said, "Damn. Now I've been rejected by my hand." She rolled over to her side and let out a long sigh. Even though she would never admit it to herself, she was pouting. She stuffed a pillow between her knees, more irritated with the feel than satisfied, and drifted off to sleep thinking about sex.

26

Her dream focused on a giant cockroach crawling its way through a pasty-white valley, stopping at the entrance of a shrub-covered cave. The cockroach turned around, produced a long black tube from its rear and extended it deep into the cave. Small white pellets squirted out of the end of the tube and became embedded in the moist, fertile soil found inside. A hand materialized within the cave, scooped up the pellets and then disappeared. Moments later, a hoard of tiny cockroaches scrambled out of the opening of the cave and climbed up out of the valley, which suddenly changed into her thighs.

Wanda started screaming, swatting at the millions of imaginary tiny bugs climbing all over her legs like maggots on a carcass. She then felt something like crumbs falling on her and tried to catch whatever it was. It was dirt. *Dirt? In her room?* Suddenly, she realized she wasn't in her room at all but in a box just big enough for her to lie in. The cockroaches had turned into worms and were boring their way into her flesh. She tried to scream again, but found her voice gone. All she managed was a long, sustained breath that sounded like air being let out of a tire.

Her sight blurred and she felt sticky goo flowing out of her ears and nose. "Is this death," she heard herself say and immediately her question was answered by a deep-throated baritone belonging to a black shape standing in the doorway of her room.

"It can be," the shape snarled.

She knew she was in her room now, but somehow it still felt like a dream. Kevin was still sleeping beside her and she tried to wake him by giving him a couple of jabs with her elbow. To her surprise her elbow past through him like a ghostly shadow and the effect frighten her. She glanced over at the night stand next to Kevin and wondered if she would be able to open the drawer and get the gun he kept in there before that dark thing could stop her. She turned to look back at the shape and discovered it had changed into a man.

In the dim, curtained light of her bedroom, she couldn't see his features, just a silhouette of an ominous-looking man in what seemed to be a... cape? She caught herself as she was about to laugh. The cape made him look like something out of a bad horror movie and it increased the illusion that she was still dreaming. The digital clock on the nightstand glowed red, but after looking at it she discovered she couldn't read the numbers. The clock face burned brightly in its perfect, geometrical way as it always had, but she was unable to fathom its meaning. Consumed by her momentary obsession with time, she forgot her intruder and was startled when he spoke.

"You are not asleep, but you are."

She turned towards the figure, feebly clutching at pillows she couldn't grab, passing through them just like Kevin.

"You are in the reality of your mind," the dark intruder intoned. "It is the only true reality that all others grow out of. The seeds of your everyday reality were placed there by false teachers and people that believe reality is the same for everyone."

Wanda gazed at the figure and became keenly aware that the figure was the same man from the bar, but he had changed somehow. It wasn't his voice or his shape—although she found it hard to tell where his body ended and his cape began. "L-L-Look," she said fighting back her fear. "I don't know who you are or how you got in here, but I'm gonna give you until the count of..." and then she couldn't think of what she was about to say. She had no concept of what it meant to count. She had a puzzled look on her face that made her seem more dim-witted than bewildered.

"Numbers mean nothing to you now nor will you find reading an ability you still possess. Those things belong in the world of the material, not in this reality, not in the world of the mind. I have come to you, Wanda, because you possess a quality of great power and strength that only a few, such as yours truly, can control. I am here to teach you of the wonders of the mind. Come! Let's take a trip in the real world." And with that, he dissolved into millions of tiny specks, each a part of the larger whole, but separate and individual. The specks coalesced into a thick, two-dimensional, vertical black line and then vanished.

Wanda lay perfectly still and wide-eyed at the sight of his form. She was beginning to become aware that she was awake in a dream of bizarre complexity. Instantly, she felt a buzzing, tingling vibration that began at the top of her head and enveloped her entire body, giving her a sense of weightlessness and free floating. She felt herself immersed in a cloud of thought and saw images flashing before her eyes in an eerie sort of dance, drawing her away from herself. She struggled against the pull and felt a dull pain coming from below her. The pain increased the harder she tried to pull away from the dancers, resulting in a tremendous release of energy from a source unknown to her. She found herself surrounded by an intense white light slowly fading into the drab hue of her bedroom. Everything was back as it was, including the ability to tell time. It was 8:15 a.m.

Wanda lay in bed on her back gripping the sheets with sweaty palms almost to the point of ripping holes in them. She was terrified. It took a few minutes for her to orientate herself to her surroundings and to assure herself, with a couple of pinches, that she was indeed awake and not in another waking dream. When she thought it was okay to move, she reached out for Kevin and found him there, snoring soundly. Usually she hated his snoring, but now it was welcome and comforting.

"Kevin, wake up. I need to talk to you." She nudged him but because she was trembling so badly the nudge turned into a rather rude shake.

"Whaa?" He stirred briefly, seemingly to claw his way out of the pit of slumber only to fall back in again without his being aware of it.

That was enough for Wanda. At least he was there and alive and real and not some creature that dissolved into nothing. She breathed a sigh of relief and rolled out of bed, falling to the floor on feeble legs. She groped for the edge of the mattress and pulled herself up to a standing position. Her head wobbled around on her neck like a spring was attached to it, dizzy and lightheaded. She thought about walking over to the other side of the bed and getting the trashcan she brought in for Kevin, but one step in that direction brought that idea to a screeching halt. She fell back against the wall and hit her head hard. The blow drove a painful spike into her already fuzzy head.

The room stopped spinning long enough for her to get to her feet, rubbing the back of her head, and she shuffled into the next room where she collapsed on the couch. Clouds of dust rose up from the impact and settled back down, causing her to sneeze. Her head pounded like she had a holiday hangover and wished she could just die and get it over with.

Wanda eyed the opened bathroom door and the shower inside, wondering if she would have the strength to make it. She decided against such a move and resigned herself to staying on the couch for the rest of her life, or until the nausea passed, whichever came first. She grabbed the remote from between the cushions, turned on the TV and surfed through a couple of channels before stopping on a talk-show dealing with incestuous rape. *Great,* she thought, rubbing her temples. *That's just what I need.* But she watched it anyway and then the one that came on after that. She watched talk-shows until late morning before daring to leave the couch.

27

The clock on the wall read 9:30 and Jason was getting anxious. The cafe had filled up considerably in the couple of hours since he and Tommy arrived. Most of the diners sat at the counter talking about the only two topics on everyone's mind: The accident at the gun store and the meeting of the night before. The former, discussed by the men, consisted of theories ranging from why Richardson killed himself to who might have wanted him dead. The latter, discussed by all, revealed that the women, borrowing a term from the younger crowd, thought he was "Hot" and the men wondered what kind of name was Beliah.

Jason fidgeted in his seat every time Tommy's father was mentioned. Occasionally, one or two would voice their opinion and then, sheepishly, look over at them, suddenly aware of Tommy's existence. Now days, Jason thought, people just didn't care about his generation or their feelings. The two of them avoided all conversation with the others and restlessly waited for 10:00 A.M.

"Another half hour and we can get out of here," Jason said, staring at the clock.

"Hey, I'm ready anytime you are," Tommy responded.

"You should have told me they were getting to you. I'm sorry. Let's get out of here and wait outside until the bookstore opens."

"Well, it's not them so much. I told you I'm pretty much over it and people are gonna talk, you know. I guess I might still be in shock or somethin'. Idda know. I'm kinda curious what people think."

"Yeah, I guess I know what you mean." *Although,* Jason thought, *you've got more balls than I have to sit here and listen while everyone knew you were here.*

"I mean we can go anytime you want to. I kinda wanted to see Missy, you know?"

"I can't believe she hasn't been around to see you or even call. After what you have been through..."

"Yeah, but some people don't know what to say in a time like this. That's why I'm glad you're my friend."

"But I'm not being much help bringing you here and letting you listen to all of this crap. These guys are jerks."

"That may be, but at least you're here with me. You kinda remind me that life goes on. I don't want anyone to feel that their life has to stop when they're around me. That makes it worst. It makes me feel like I'm the cause of what happened. Sure it hurts, but I'll get over it. And as soon as people let me have my pain and experience it my way, the sooner I can get back in the middle of things. I can't when people give me funny looks and tell me how I feel. How do they know?" Tommy's tone started filling with anger and he got louder with each passing word.

"My father died, not theirs. And if I don't want to cry about it, then I shouldn't have to. Who's to say my form of grief is more wrong than anyone else's? Huh?"

"Hey, I know what you mean. I mean, I hear what you're saying. I mean..." Jason was at a loss for words. Listening to Tommy vent, Jason sat in awe of his friend and his mature outlook on death. Jason couldn't figure out why Tommy valued their relationship so much. If it was his dad that died he knew he wouldn't have been able to accept it as well as Tommy in so short of a time. But now, Jason saw the pain coming out. Tommy wasn't the superman Jason thought he might be. Tommy was, after all, human.

"Ah, forget it. I'm just ticked at Missy for not comin' over."

Tommy was calming down, much to Jason's relief, and he took the opportunity to suggest leaving. Besides, it was already past 10:00. "Come on," he said, standing up. "Let's get out of here. Lazenby's open and I'm sure Missy's gonna be there."

"Yeah, she's supposed to work all day. I hope Mr. Lazenby let's her talk to me for a little while. Damn, I was supposed to help him today."

"I'm sure he'll understand. He's an okay guy," Jason paused, remembering the time Mr. Lazenby pushed Tommy off his porch because he brought Missy home late. "Well, sometimes."

They stared at each other, seemingly thinking the same thing and broke out in a good hardy laugh. They left the cafe with the diners wondering if they were crazy.

"I betcha they did it," Jason heard one of the diners say as the door clicked closed behind them. He doubted if Tommy heard it and that was okay by him.

28

Lazenby's was just a few doors down from the cafe and the two walked there in friendly silence. Tonka, having wandered away, came back and discovered his master gone from the cafe. In a momentary state of panic, he dropped his nose to the ground and followed the trail of his master and the "other one". After a few moments he spotted the objects of his hunt. Stopping, he crouched down, front paws forward, hind legs tensed as if ready to pounce, and took off after his master. To a casual observer, Jason and Tommy would have been in the path of a rabid dog. Tonka closed the gap between him and his target and sailed through the air, landing on all fours just behind Jason and playfully mouthed his master's hand.

"Tonka! Knock it off. Not now." Jason was caught off guard and his reaction was one of surprise rather than true anger.

"He scared the piss out of me. I didn't even hear him comin'." Tommy stood a couple of feet away with one hand to his chest and the other scratching the back of his head.

Jason, laughing now, caught their reflection in the large front window of the dry cleaners and saw Tommy from the view of a spectator. He glanced down at the reflected Tommy and noticed a small wet circle in the crotch of his pants. That made him laugh even harder. With tears streaming down his eyes, Jason turned around to face Tommy. He wanted desperately to point out the stain, but stopped when he saw a raven-haired woman driving a red pick up heading in the same direction as they.

Jason darted off after the truck leaving Tommy behind. Tonka, thinking it was another game, chased after him. Jason leaned forward, craning his neck, trying to get a better look at the driver, but she was driving faster than he could run. Casually, the driver turned and looked directly at him, their eyes locking for a moment, and then the moment passed. As she turned onto Route Nine and out of town, Jason managed to snag where the driver called home. The license plate read: Florida.

"Hey," Tommy said breathlessly, running up behind him. "Wha... what are you doing? If you wanted to race to Lazenby's, you could have given me a clue."

"No, it was that truck. Did you see it? The one with the Florida tags. Tonka get down."

"The red one? What about it?"

"The driver—she's a redhead."

"Good lookin', huh?"

"Yeah, I guess, I mean, she was the one from my dreams. You know the weird ones I have. That was her, I'm sure of it."

"Really? You mean the one you float around with, the red-haired girl?"

Yeah, yeah. She looked right at me. In my dreams she's prettier somehow, but that was her. I'll never forget that face." Jason stood in amazement looking at some inner mental picture. "That was her," he said. "I'm sure of it."

He was also sure but unable—or maybe unwilling—to explain to Tommy that the woman had a glow about her. Something seemed to radiate from her that reminded him of his dreams. He thought that maybe his mind was just comparing the two pictures, the one from his dreams and the one just now, and superimposed them, but he quickly discarded that. He knew he saw light all around her; it blazed in a hazy, sun-blinding way that was pleasant to look at.

"Come on," Tommy said, grabbing Jason's shoulder. "She's gone now and Beliah's waiting."

Jason had forgotten all about the book signing and the remark hit him like a slap in the face. He blinked several times and shook his head trying to refocus, and remember why he was there in the first place. "Beliah? Oh, yeah."

Tommy reached the door first and saw through the glass Mr. Lazenby slamming books down and making a lot of noise. He was clearly upset at something.

"What's eating him, you think?" Jason looked at Tommy and he returned the question with a shrug.

"Who knows? All I know is that I haven't seen Missy since day before yesterday and then only for a minute. I couldn't have pissed him off."

"Tonka," Jason said. "Stay out here and keep out of trouble. We'll be right back." They opened the door cautiously and tried to be as inconspicuous as possible.

"Tommy!" Mr. Lazenby growled.

"Yes, sir?"

"I thought you were going steady with my Missy."

"Yes sir, I am, or at least I was yesterday." Tommy shook nervously and Jason was surprised that Mr. Lazenby didn't even seem the least bit concerned about Tommy or his father.

"Then why don't you keep a tight rein on her. I was seeing red early this morning on account of her. I thought you kept her out all night. I was going to beat the hell out of you when I got a hold of you. Oh!" Lazenby's tone changed from anger to almost humility. "I'm sorry about your dad. Matt was a good man."

"Thanks, I'm gonna miss him." Then, "You say Missy was out all night?"

"Daddy!"

All three turned in the direction of the voice and stared at a girl that sounded like Missy but had a much lower, huskier voice. She looked like Missy, but had more of a luscious, seductive manner; and dressed, well, Jason and Tommy stood with their eyes glued to her body, their mouths hanging open. She was wearing a tight, white-cotton halter-top that began and ended on her breasts, a short-short black mini skirt that barely covered her private area, and three-inch spike-heeled shoes that gave her walk a pleasing and sexy gait. Jason didn't think she had any panties on and became quite embarrassed when she caught him staring at the bottom of her skirt.

"Daddy, I told you I wanted to tell Tommy that. You make it sound so baaaad," she pouted.

"I thought I told you to put some clothes on. If the preacher comes in here, I don't know what I would do."

"But daddy," she said, pouting even more. "I like the way I'm dressed. Don't you Tommy?" She strutted over to Tommy and put her arms around his neck, giving him a hard kiss on the mouth.

"M-M-M-Missy? What gives?"

"Why don't we go in the back and I'll tell you all about it." She grabbed Tommy by a belt loop and led him through the shelving of books into the back.

With Tommy and Missy gone, Jason was at a loss to say anything to Mr. Lazenby. What can you say, he thought, to a man whose daughter changed overnight from a prick tease in schoolgirl dress to someone that should be soliciting on a street corner? Jason found himself unable to open his mouth and it was just as well, for Lazenby went back to slamming books and mumbling to himself.

Jason wandered around the fair-sized bookstore searching for Beliah. He saw a small table and chair off to the side that he assumed Beliah would use and the box of books he would sign, but no Beliah. He glanced at the clock on the far wall. It hung over the door to the back room Missy and Tommy just went through. It read: 10:16.

He walked up and down six rows of shelving, each containing a different category of book. He passed the westerns, the romance, the sci-fi, the how-to, and then stopped at the philosophy/occult section. He smiled to himself. It struck him funny that Lazenby would put those two completely different genres together. Then he thought about it for a moment. They were both, basically, nothing but a set of beliefs. Even the religious section right next to them was based on belief. An inquisitive frown formed on his face and he nodded in agreement. It made sense to him now.

His eye caught the row of books that a few days earlier he had browsed through and found, much to his amazement, the same two books he had recently purchased. It wasn't that they were there—this was, after all, a bookstore—but that Lazenby had reordered and received them back so quickly. Normally, when Jason special-ordered something, it took a month or more, but this hadn't even been a week. He shrugged resigning himself to the fact the he would never understand the book business.

Jason looked over at the back room. It was barely visible through the bookshelves. *They've been in there ten minutes. What are they doing?* Then a lewd smile spread across his face and he knew exactly what they were doing. How could Tommy keep his hands off of her? Jason knew he didn't want to be alone with her. Tommy was his friend and he didn't want to see if his friendship was strong enough to overcome his teenage lust. He was sure it would be, but just in case he wouldn't follow Missy into any enclosed rooms without Tommy. Suddenly, he was jolted out of his thoughts by the sound of a barking dog, his barking dog. He thought how easy and quickly it was for him to distinguish that sound as being his dog and wondered if he was "seeing" like a blind person. He figured he was.

"Jason!" It was Lazenby. "Come get your damn dog before he rips Beliah apart."

Jason ran to the front of the store and flew outside the door, sailing over the steps and landing solidly on the sidewalk. Tonka had Beliah backed against the wall of the post office, the dog's head lowered between his shoulders, growling, ready to attack. Beliah stood pressed against the red brick wall with his hands, palms facing out, extended in front of him in an effort to ward off any attack.

"Tonka!" Jason screamed, but the dog continued to inch forward with his eyes locked on Beliah.

"Get this dog away from me before I have to hurt it," Beliah said in an eerily calm voice.

Jason took that remark a little too personal. *Like you're in a position to hurt anyone,* he thought. But the tone of Beliah's voice and the confidence it projected worried Jason. Maybe Beliah could hurt him. Maybe he had a gun or a knife. Jason quickly looked for any bulges on Beliah that would indicate a weapon of some sort, but didn't see any. Of course, that doesn't mean anything. If Beliah wanted to press charges, Tonka could be locked up at least for the rest of the weekend if not longer, and Jason knew Beliah knew that, too.

"Yeah, I'm sorry. I don't know what his problem is. He's never done this before." And that was the truth. He approached Tonka from behind and grabbed him around the neck. He didn't wear a collar and never had, mainly because Jason didn't see the need for one. Besides, most people knew his dog and liked him. This was something new.

Jason wrapped his arms tightly around Tonka's neck to stop his forward movement. The dog's muscles were popping out all over the place and it reminded Jason of a cartoon where one of the characters swallowed a strength pill and ballooned into Arnold Schwarzenegger. He could see veins sticking out the sides of his rear legs, pulsating in time with his heartbeat. Tonka's considerable chest was made larger by his slow, deep breathing. He didn't think Tonka had it in him to be like this. Jason had never seen his dog like this and he was scared.

The bell on the door of the bookstore sounded and Jason turned to see a frazzled Tommy flying down the steps, breathless and wide-eyed. Jason saw that Tommy was just as surprised and puzzled as he.

"What happened?" Tommy said, wiping sweat or slobber from his mouth with the back of his hand.

"I don't know. He's never done this before." Jason pulled his arm tighter around Tonka's neck. "C'mon, boy. Back off. It's okay."

"Hey mister," Tommy said, glancing sideways at Beliah, "Why don'cha go inside. I think we hav'em."

"Thinking can get that dog hurt," Beliah said with his hands now resting on his hips.

"We've got'em. Just you go. I wouldn't want to be responsible for this dog ripping your balls of," Tommy snapped.

Obviously, Tommy took offense at Beliah's confidence, too. "He didn't mean that mister," Jason quickly added. "He wouldn't hurt a bug. I promise."

Beliah sidestepped the group and walked causally up the steps towards the door.

"I'm sorry, mister. I didn't—"

"Well, if you're really sorry come buy my book." Beliah smiled at him with what appeared to be a genuine look of sincerity.

"Sure... I mean, yeah. I was going to anyway." Jason was relieved that Beliah didn't seem to harbor any ill will against Tonka, but he was more afraid of what Sheriff Dunn would say if he found out. The Sheriff had warned Jason before about his dog running wild without a lease and he could just hear it now. Tonka would have to be destroyed because in the four years of his life he attacked one stranger. Jason shuddered at the thought and gripped his dog tighter.

That did it. Tonka relaxed completely and started licking Jason on the side of his face. He maneuvered around to the front of his dog not quite sure if he should release him yet. Tommy reached down and playfully patted the dog's belly. Jason, meanwhile, rubbed Tonka's muzzle, pulling his jowls up over his teeth the way he liked it. He was visibly relieved that the ordeal was over.

"He's okay, aren't you boy?" Jason said, popping him across the nose and getting into a fighters' stance, looking like he was ready to fight. To an outsider, that pop looked to be cruel and maybe dangerous, provoking a return of the beast from hell that possessed the dog a few moments ago. But to Jason and his dog, it was play-time.

Tonka leaped at Jason and caught a finger with his mouth. He gnawed and slobbered all over it for a few seconds and then let go. Jason looked up and saw Tommy watching the scene. He appeared quite pleased to see the two so engaged.

Tommy turned his head to look over his shoulder, making sure Beliah was inside, and then asked, "What do you think?"

"I don't really know. He could've teased him. Hell, I've never seen him like that."

"It scared me I don't mind tellin' ya."

"Yeah, me too. Say, what were you two doing in the back for so long?"

Tommy smiled so large that Jason thought the top of his head would fall off. "We did it!"

"Did what?"

"You know what I'm talkin' about."

"What—rearranged the files? What?"

"You son-of-a-bitch: IT! We did IT! She gave it up right on top of her old man's desk."

"You've got to be kidding? All right!" Jason raised one hand in the air and Tommy slapped it.

"Yeah. She said she didn't know what to say to me about my dad and figured the best thing was to show me how she felt. I'll tell you what, she must really care."

"You're the first, ole buddy."

"And the last," Tommy said with a bright, mischievous smile. "You better believe it."

"Yeah, you bet." But Jason didn't believe it. If there was one thing he knew more about than Tommy, it was sex. He had lost his virginity years ago, back when he was fourteen. He had lost it to a twenty-year-old "college girl". Her name was Lori and they met while she was home on break. Because of their age difference Jason didn't think she even knew who he was. She was driving a Camaro and he was pushing a bicycle with a flat tire. She stopped and offered him a ride and he took it.

They got to talking and Lori couldn't get off of the topic of sex. It embarrassed Jason to even think about it in the way she so casually spoke about it. She told him of all the beer parties and the sex that went on in college. Jason got the opinion that was all you did in college was drink beer and get laid. He liked the idea and gave second thoughts to attending.

She didn't take him directly to his house, which was fine by him, but cruised around the back-country roads talking about sex and drinking. They stopped at a store to buy a six-pack of something and drove away drinking and talking about drinking and sex. After about two beers Jason was lit and he found a self-assured boldness within him he didn't know existed. He started talking about how he wanted to have sex, but all the girls he knew wouldn't give it up. She understood and said that girls in this town were brainwashed by the preacher every Sunday and that in the "Real world" everybody had sex.

With the day coming to a close and dusk settling in they drove back to town and parked behind the hotel. The beers were gone and it was Jason that brought up sex again. Drunk as he was on his three beers, he was becoming very brazen. He suggested that boys were usually better at sex than girls because they started earlier, either engaged in the real thing or in practice. Lori found that comment funny and Jason asked her if she wanted him to prove it. She said yes and the two of them "did it", as Tommy would say, in the back of the Camaro. He remembered it being really difficult to get in a position where both of them could enjoy it.

They finished up in less than five minutes and Lori seemed especially embarrassed, unable to say anything as she drove him home. He thanked her for a wonderful time and she shrugged. He asked her if he could see her again before she left and she snorted. He got out of the car and quickly unloaded his bike, which was sticking out of the tiny trunk, and then she drove off, leaving him standing in the middle of the road waving to a cloud of dust.

He never told anyone what had happened, not even Tommy. He figured no one would believe him anyway and maybe that was okay. He lost his virginity to a woman and whether anyone knew it or not, he knew.

He also knew, while listening to Tommy blabbing about him being the first and last, that Missy had that same look in her eye that Lori had four years ago: Lust. Once you get that look, he thought, you'll do anyone. He felt sorry for his friend, but not too sorry. Tommy would always be the first and nothing could change that. Tommy, Jason knew, was in love with Missy and no matter what happened she would always hold a special memory of him.

"C'mon," Jason said. "Let's go see Beliah."

29

Jason practically ran into the rear of the truck when he turned around. "When did that get here?"

"What, the truck? Idda know. Who cares?" Tommy stopped at the door looking very impatient. "I wanna go see Missy."

Jason examined the license plate to be sure of what he thought. There, hanging just below the chrome bumper, was his answer. "Florida," he said aloud and ran up the steps into the bookstore. "Tonka, stay here."

Tonka lifted his leg and put his mark on the pickup.

Jason entered and scanned the store, hoping to see the owner of the truck. His entry drew everybody's attention: Lazenby, behind the counter, stopped counting money; Tommy, unseen behind a row of books, stopped fondling Missy's breasts; Missy stopped letting him; and Beliah, sitting at a table stacked with books, studied him intently.

It was Beliah who was the first to speak. "That dog chasing you, man?"

"What? No, I thought I saw somethin'. Forget it."

"I wonder about you boy," Lazenby said. His mood had brightened considerably.

"Hey man," Beliah said, "I think you owe me for not turning your dog in. What do you say?" He was grinning.

"Sure, mister."

"Call me Beliah," he said, standing up and extending a welcoming hand. "My friends do. That's some dog you got there."

"Yeah, he's a mess. I don't know what got into him. I'm real sorry."

Jason took and released Beliah's hand, giving it the customary pump. That's when he noticed a small medallion hanging around Beliah's neck. It was tied there with a piece of leather string and hung about mid chest. It was bronze in color and round, about the size of a silver dollar, with a triangle and a rising sun embossed in the center. There was writing that Jason could barely make out, and as he tried Beliah noticed him staring.

"You like this?" he asked, pointing to the medallion with a well-manicured finger.

"I didn't mean to stare," he said, diverting his eyes. "I was just looking at it." Jason felt like a kid who had gotten caught playing with daddy's gun.

"That's okay. You were trying to read it, weren't you?"

"Yeah." Jason looked back at the medallion and he saw what he thought was a purplish glow coming from the imprinted sun. He blinked, wondering if it was some kind of trick caused by the light in the store. When that didn't work, he moved his head slightly to see if it changed. It didn't.

"It reads: 'Creation' at the top here," Beliah said, pointing without looking. "Along the base of the triangle it reads 'Belief', with 'Power' and 'Force' making up the sides. Do you see it?" That last was said in a raspy, gravelly voice.

"See what?" Jason didn't know if he was talking about the light or not.

"The words, man. Can you see the words?"

"Yeah, but what does it mean? The medallion, I mean."

Beliah had seated himself again and leaned back in the chair, pushing himself away from the table. Missy and Tommy walked over to see what Jason and Beliah were talking about and even Lazenby appeared to be listening while counting his money. They were the only ones in the bookstore, making Beliah the center of attention.

Tommy was leaning against a book table and held Missy close against him. Missy was eyeing Beliah with the same look Jason had seen her give Tommy just before they went into the back room. The look made Jason wonder if Tommy's first lay was already checking out new ground. He turned back to Beliah and saw him looking at Missy the same way. Tommy, it seemed, was oblivious to the sexual communication being carried out right before him. He's got a hard-on, Jason thought, and can't see pass it. She's gonna do him wrong.

The exchange between the two was brief but definite. He regarded Missy now as a slut in heat. Jason knew he couldn't blame Beliah, though. After all, he was human and just look at the way she was dressed! *If it wasn't for Tommy, I'd have a go of her,* he prided himself. Jason didn't trust her anymore. There was something not right about her. Her look was definitely sexy, but also evil in some way that Jason couldn't put his finger on. He didn't know why he thought that but it was there all the same.

"Belief," Beliah said, pulling his eyes away from Missy, "is the foundation of all Creation, hence the base of the triangle. With belief, one gets power over his life and with that power, one can generate a force. The three together can change Creation, or Reality, into whatever one wants."

"Force? You mean like on Star Wars?" Jason stared at the medallion again, but this time the sun wasn't glowing.

"Not exactly. That's the movies, this is real life. The Force I'm talking about is the essence of all things that each and every one of us has contact with. It's what makes you continue when you don't have the strength to. It's the motivation and the courage that pushes you along. Most people don't realize they are actually in control of that force. The ones that do recognize their potential, those are the ones who rise to the top."

"It sounds 'New-Age' to me," Lazenby said, still counting money.

"If you believe that we are coming into a New Age of Man, well, then it is. With the dawning of the twenty-first century, the future is now."

Beliah had everyone listening. Even Tommy had stopped his gyrating against Missy long enough to cool off and Missy looked more interested in what Beliah was saying than giving him that lustful look. Jason, too, was fascinated by what he was hearing. Beliah, it seemed to Jason, had an almost mesmerizing effect on those around him. He was like a narcotic slowly gaining the trust of the user until it was too late and the effect became permanent. Jason listened intently, but somewhere in the back of his mind he heard a voice—a voice from one of his dreams maybe?—calling out to him.

"Beware the yeast of the Pharisee," the voice said.

No, Jason thought, the voice wasn't from one of his dreams. That phrase was something he knew from Sunday school. He didn't know exactly what it meant then and he sure as hell didn't know what it meant now.

"Don't you know that a little yeast will contaminate the whole loaf?" the voice said.

Jason was struck with the illusion that the world was moving in slow motion and he was in the center of it. Beliah smiled and the corners of his mouth gradually peeled back, revealing fangs sharper and more plentiful than those in Tonka's mouth. His nose grew and curved down, stopping over the tip of his chin. His eyes were pulled back and up from the sides, giving him a distinct, over-exaggerated, oriental appearance. His eyebrows had a distinct upward slant.

Jason reeled back in horror and fell into the counter. He felt a hand on his shoulder and looked back to see Lazenby, only this Lazenby was a mirror image of the freak Beliah had become. He screamed and knocked Lazenby's hand away, his arms waving wildly in the air.

"Jason, what's wrong?" It was Tommy.

Jason looked at his friend wondering why he didn't see what was happening to Beliah and Missy's father. What he saw though was the same hideous transformation consuming both Tommy and Missy. He screamed again and Tommy and Missy twisted around to look at each other. Missy's mouth opened and a black, snake-like tongue shot out and wrapped around Tommy's tongue in a grotesque, perverted scene that Jason could only describe as some obscene sexual act. He screamed for the third time and shut his eyes tight against the images.

"Jason?"

He heard Tommy's voice but was afraid to open his eyes, thinking that if the images remained he was out the door. Jason cautiously opened his eyes and saw sanity. He stared directly at Tommy.

"Are you okay, buddy?" There was real concern in Tommy's voice. "What's up?"

Jason relaxed a bit totally unaware that he had been clenching his teeth. Everything was back to normal.

"Boy, you on drugs or somethin'?" Lazenby asked.

"No, I..." Jason was at a loss of what to say.

"Maybe it was something I said." Beliah remarked amusingly.

Missy giggled at that and Jason shot her a hard look that caused her to recoil back into Tommy. She immediately lost all of her sensuous appeal and instead looked like a frighten, little, seventeen-year-old girl clinging to her boyfriend for protection.

"C'mon, Jason. What gives?" Tommy's voice had a decidedly sharp edge to it.

Jason locked eyes with Tommy unsure if he was a friend or a foe. Tommy's eyes remained firmly on Jason's but with puzzled concern behind them. Jason's eyes soften, followed by the rest of his body. Leaning against a bookshelf, Jason rubbed the palms of his hands in his eyes and rested them there for a moment before lowering them.

Tommy pried himself away from Missy and walked over to Jason. "Are you okay?" he asked, putting a hand on his shoulder.

"Yeah, I'm sorry. It's the... I think it was..." and then he lowered his voice so no one could hear but Tommy, "one of my dreams. I think I had a waking dream."

"Do you need to lie down or somethin'?" Tommy whispered back.

Jason shook his head and spoke in a normal tone, "No, I must have gotten a bad piece of sausage at the cafe this morning."

"I thought I was the only one," Beliah said.

Jason smiled and then started laughing. Instantly, the store was filled with laughter and Jason pushed whatever happened to the back of his mind. He didn't really know what happened and he definitely didn't feel he could explain what had happened, much less deal with it. The laughing made him feel better.

"Next time you want me to shut up, just ask," Beliah said grinning at him.

Jason realized that Beliah's smile carried that same narcotic effect that his talking had, frightening, yet comforting. He decided he didn't like Beliah, but if asked he couldn't say why.

"Are you filling these town folk with more of your lies, Beliah?"

All eyes turned toward the front door to see who spoke. The voice belonged to a tall, crimson-haired woman with brilliant emerald-green eyes. She was well-proportioned and overly endowed, like Missy, but not over balanced. Her tight-fitting jeans filled out nicely and accented a flannel, button down shirt tucked inside her jeans. Her thick, straight red mane hung over her left shoulder, held together with a denim wrap. She stood with one leg out in front and hands resting on her hips in a "Come if you dare!" way. Her breathy, feminine voice was gentle, yet conveyed a command of authority. Over all, this woman looked beautiful and sounded intimidating.

"You're her," Jason said incredulously, wide-eyed, his chin resting against his chest. "You're the one from my dreams."

"I'll take that as a compliment," she casually replied as she strolled into the store, glancing about the place and smiling at Jason before turning to Beliah.

"Tamara, my dear girl. And what, may I ask, are you doing here?"

She glanced at the medallion around Beliah's neck, shaking her head. "You still wear that?"

Jason looked at Tommy and he mouthed "That's her!" which Tommy returned with his own silent, disbelieving, "Really?" Missy was gawking at Tamara with a cross between hate and envy and Lazenby had a great big grin plastered across his face. He was watching Tamara's hips as she shifted her weight from one foot to the other.

"That's not answering the question," Beliah said smoothly. "Did you come to buy my book?"

"No, I don't buy garbage. I just wanted you to know I was here, that's all."

"Yes, I felt you."

Jason's ears perked up. *Felt you*, did he say?

"But that doesn't interest me right now," Beliah continued. "I have a book signing in progress, as you can see."

"Watch your dreams, Beliah. I'll be seeing you." With that, she spun around and caught Lazenby staring at her. She threw a humorous look at him and said, "See something you like?"

"I... Um... I wasn't—"

"Save it," she said, wiggling back across the floor and heading out to leave. She stopped next to Jason and touched his cheek gently, almost lovingly with the back of one finger, then whispered, "We'll talk. Just remember that light you saw." She turned again and looked straight at Beliah.

Light, what light? Jason looked at Beliah, then back to Tamara. Was she talking about the light in his dreams or, No! She must have been talking about the light from the medallion. Jason looked at Beliah again and saw him leaning back in his swivel chair, playing with the medallion between his fingers. He heard the door close and looked over his shoulder, barely catching Tamara's profile as she moved out of sight. He heard the roar of a powerful engine and the meshing of gears. Jason darted out of the store just in time to see her peel out of the parking lot, turning right and heading up Route Nine.

"Forget it kid," Jason heard from over his shoulder. "She's way out of your league." It was Lazenby, who had followed behind him. "Hell, she's probably out of my league."

They returned to the store and Jason grabbed the one of the books off the stacked table. "Will you sign this, please?"

"Sure, Jason," Beliah said, taking the book from his hand. He scribbled something on the first page and handed it back to him. "There you go. Let me know what you think, okay?"

"S-S-Sure." Jason took the book, trying hard not to look Beliah in the eyes or at the medallion around his neck. Ever since he walked in here weird things had happened. He quickly reviewed them and remembered it started with Missy's appearance and ended with Tamara, the girl from his dreams. Something just wasn't right.

He opened the book and read the inscription: "Watch out for dreams, they can kill you! The Devil." Jason was taken aback and blinked wildly. Then the inscription changed and read: "Take your dreams seriously; they might come true! Beliah." Jason peered over the top of the book and saw Beliah smiling at him in that same narcotic way. He snapped the book closed and moved over to Tommy and Missy.

"He signed it?" Tommy asked between gropes.

"Yeah, he—" Jason noticed a self-conscious grin on Tommy's face and then on Missy's. They were spooning each other with her back to his front and Tommy leaning against a shelf. Missy had her hands behind her back, obviously kneading his crotch. Jason glanced over at Lazenby and discovered the view was partially blocked by the bookshelves.

"What?" Tommy asked smiling.

"Nothing. Hey, I'm takin' off. You comin'?

"Uh, no. I think I'm gonna stay around and help Missy. Besides, I want to see who comes in."

"Yeah, okay." Then looking directly at Missy he said, "You could at least stop that while I'm talking to him."

Missy smiled that seductive grin again and asked, "Why, you jealous?"

"What's wrong, Jaaason," Tommy teased. "Can't I have a little fun, too? After all, you've got a dream girl."

That stung. Jason stared at Tommy and wondered if he had told Missy anything about his dreams. He searched his face for some clue and didn't find any. Jason didn't like Tommy's attitude. As long as Missy had a grip on his privates, he thought, he'll only be thinking with the head between his legs. Jason turned to leave and said, "Look, I gotta go. See ya."

"Aw, don't go away mad," Tommy pleaded.

"Yeah, just go away."

Jason spun around, ready to cram his fist down Missy's throat. What he found, though, was Tommy and her in a lip lock that made him wonder if she really did say anything. After a few moments, he stormed out of the store wanting nothing but to go home. It had been a weird morning.

CHAPTER 6

Our individual lives touch and interact with each other. Just by our existence, we start a chain reaction that is beyond our present comprehension. To change the world, we must change our own lives. The stronger the influence we have over other people, the more change we can make. Good or bad.
From The Book of Beliah
Verse 6

30

PHIL HARTMAN FOUND HIMSELF TURNED upside down with his neck bent at a severe angle. His head was trapped between his right shoulder and the roof of the car. He knew what had happened. Ironically, he remembered telling Dunn that Hope needed to post a speed limit sign right before the same turn he just missed.

The pressure on his neck was excruciating and he wondered how it was that he was still alive. He took a quick inventory of his body and found the only other part of it trapped was his right arm. It was caught between the bench seat of the cruiser and the crushed roof at an angle that pushed his right shoulder up and his head sideways. He tried to move his head and found the answer to why his neck wasn't broken: The headrest had supported most of the weight of the roof when the car had rolled over.

Seeing everything upside down Phil tried to make sense of the situation and considered a possible means of escape. The car had rolled over on its roof and then came to rest slightly more to the passenger side. He decided that if he pushed with his feet he might be able to pop a portion of the roof back into shape, thus freeing his head and giving him use of his arm.

Phil pressed his head as far as possible into his shoulder and extended his legs. He thought of his high-school days in the weight room doing squats, pushing with the same intensity as he did then trying to lift 300 pounds. The roof gave briefly, but then quit. He stopped and rested a few moments and tried again. The roof moved again, but instead of stopping it bent outward.

With the pressure released from his neck he was able to bring his left arm around so that it rested underneath the steering wheel and that supported some of his weight. He felt the shift in pressure in his trapped shoulder and knew that if he didn't free it, it would soon be dislocated. Phil discovered he was able to move his right arm below the elbow and he used the opportunity to search the back seat for anything that might help his situation. (Because of the collision, the rear seat was up against the back of the front seat and all of the items there were within his reach.) He touched the shotgun that had come out of its cradle, an extra pair of handcuffs, and a baton. He grabbed the baton and the feel brought back the horrible memory of Angie. He had forgotten why he was out here in the first place and the back of his eyes prickled with tears. He fought them back and told himself that his only chance for survival was to free himself and take care of his unfinished business before anyone found him.

He managed to flip the baton over in his hand and worked it between the seat and roof. He pumped the baton like a lever, using the seat as the fulcrum. Jacking it like a tire iron, he was able to gain enough room to wiggle his arm out. The freedom landed him fully against the roof and positioned his head just inches away from the dash. With both hands and arms free, Phil twisted his body and crawled across the roof and out of the broken passenger window.

He stood up and splinters of pain raced down his back. He put his left hand to the small of his back, cursing. The pain subsided somewhat and he walked to the rear of the car. Angie's body lay a few feet away from it still rolled up in the blood-soaked blanket. He fought back a momentary turn of his stomach and searched the opened trunk for the shovel he knew must be there.

A vehicle drove by and the sound startled him, causing him to bump his head on the back of the trunk. His heart skipped a beat at the sound of brakes, fearing someone had seen him, and then realized they were braking for the turn. He recovered, although his heart was hammering away inside his chest, and managed to catch a glimpse of a red pickup rounding the turn and heading away from town.

He was unable to locate the shovel in the trunk, putting his head up inside and probing around with his hands. A quick search of the surrounding area convinced him that it must still be somewhere in the car. He yanked on the passenger door, trying to get it open, and the car shifted its weight towards him. He stretched out his arms in an attempt to steady it. After a few moments of acting like a brace, he decided the car was stable and continued searching the interior for the shovel. "It's gotta be in here," he said. "There's no way Dunn would let a cruiser out without all assigned equipment." Then, in the back of his mind, he heard, "But that's your job, silly Philly."

Phil spun around expecting to see someone, but found he was all alone. He leaned back in the cruiser and the voice spoke again.

"Why don't you go and play with your willy?"

"Who said that?" Phil asked the surrounding trees.

"Ain't nobody here but us murderers and crazies, and a queer or two."

Phil clamped his hands over his ears and screamed. "Leave me alone. What do you want from me?"

"I only want you to succeed in burying that whore," the voice said softly. "With all of the screaming you're doing, you're going to attract attention."

"Yeah, yeah." Phil looked around, simultaneously searching for the owner of the voice and seeing if he had indeed attracted the attention of a "someone". There were a lot of drifters in these parts, he knew. They would pass through town from somewhere and go through these woods on the way to the river. Several times a year Phil and Dunn had to come and chased them away from camping on the lake. During the summer months it became a weekly thing.

"Get the shovel, Phil. It's in the car. You know it's in the car. Check under the seats. Sheriff Cow Dung probably put it under the seat."

"The seat! Yeah, that's where it is." Phil stopped wondering who owned the voice and started to accept the help he was being given. He reached in the cruiser and felt around the underside of the seat. He found a package and latched onto it. Pulling it out, the package got hung up on a broken seat spring and a sharp coil of wire dug into it. He pushed the package back with one hand and then grabbed the broken spring. The package was now free and virtually fell out of his hand and onto the ground. Without thinking, he released the tension on the broken coil wire, causing it to spring back, penetrating the palm of his left hand.

Phil suppressed a scream, wrenching his hand away, and ripped the flesh even more. He held the wrist of his injured hand as blood gushed out in a reddish-purple torrent that covered both arms to his elbows. He caught a glimpse of himself in the polished black fender of his car and saw his face had turned a frightening shade of alabaster. His head started swimming and images flew before his eyes of what had happened over the last twelve hours. He knew he was on the edge of total blackout when that voice spoke again and the message centered him back in this reality.

"Snap out of it, Philly. For crying out loud, it's just a scratch. It's not like you lost your hand."

Phil examined the back of his hand, staring at the bones and muscles laid out in plain view. He wiggled his fingers and giggled insanely as he observed the tendons working in conjunction with the muscles.

"What did I tell you, Philly? Everything works. Now pick up that shovel and get busy digging a hole for that slut. DO IT NOW!"

That last was given with such force that Phil jumped back, cartwheeling his arms to keep his balance. He picked up the plastic, triangular package, which was more of a carrying pouch, and unsnapped the flap at one end. He pulled out a standard, army-issue "E-Tool". The shovel was folded in thirds, the handle breaking down in two places and the head making up the triangular shape of the pouch. With one quick jerk, the E-tool snapped together forming a three-foot shovel with one side of the blade equipped with a serrated edge.

Phil went over to the body, knelt down and lifted it into his arms. He hoisted it on one shoulder and humped through a break in the trees to a clearing several yards away from the wreckage. Dropping his bundle with a sickening squish, he dug a shallow grave and dumped the body in. Sweat rolled down his face and he wiped his brow with his injured hand. The salt from the sweat ignited an explosion of pain that reverberated up his arm and into his chest. He held back a scream and stood gritting his teeth, shaking.

"Not bad, Philly," the inner voice soothed. "You're getting better at handling it. You're stronger than I thought."

Phil's eyes grew wide and his lips curled away from his teeth giving him a psychotic look, smiling the smile of a madman. The pain dumped adrenalin into his blood stream and filled him with a strength that he hungrily gulped down. He checked his hand again and noticed dirt had found its way into the gash. The area immediately around the wound was painfully swollen and dirty. The last rational part of his mind spoke to him calmly, saying, "That is a serious wound, Phil. You have to go get help before infection sets in."

Phil used his shirt to wipe most of the dirt away from around the wound and a worried expression crossed his face. "I'm gonna die. Wonder if it gets infected?"

"No you're not, Philly. I won't let you. Just get rid of the infection."

"Yeah, but how?"

"You know how, Philly. You have to cut it out. Cut the infection out of your body. Cut it off before it's too late."

Panic raced through him at the thought, but he grabbed the shovel anyway and ran a finger down the saw-toothed edge.

"Use it like an axe, Philly. It'll hurt, but think about the strength you'll receive. If salt in a wound can make you strong imagine what this will feel like."

Phil deliberately hit his hand with the flat side of the shovel. He hissed at the pain and an almost ecstatic smile covered his face. The rush of adrenalin was like food for his soul and he relished it. The pain soon faded away and Phil made up his mind about what to do with the festering, pus-filled flesh he called a hand. "I'll just bury it with Angie, a reminder to her in hell of who did this." In the black pit of his poisoned heart, Phil didn't care who actually killed her because he wanted the credit all the same.

He went over to the car and laid his hand on the chrome bumper, giggling like a nervous schoolgirl. He raised the shovel above his head and swung it, serrated edge down, on his wrist, repeatedly, laughing louder with every blow.

31

The phone rang and Sheriff Dunn picked it up. "Yeah, Sheriff's office."

"This is Shrader over at the Hotel," the caller said. "I think you need to come over here, right now."

"What seems to be the problem?"

"I think it would be better if I showed you."

Dunn pulled the phone away from his ear and peered at the receiver with a queer look in his eyes. Shrader sounded a little dazed and overwhelmed, not at all like the man Dunn had known for years. "Sure, Bill. Just give me an hour or so to finish—"

Bill cut him off, sounding overly anxious. "You have to come now, Sheriff. There's been a... an accident. Somebody's been killed."

"I'll be right there. Don't touch a thing, and for God's sake don't tell anyone." Dunn dropped the phone in its cradle and went to his desk. Pulling open one of the drawers, he grabbed the pistol laying there and checked the butt for a magazine: it was missing. The pistol was a Nine mm Glock, the kind made in Austria, and his personal choice. He reached back in the drawer and found a twenty round, fully loaded magazine. He snatched it up and studied the tip of the first round. It was partially hollow with a point recessed in the center. Dunn slammed the clip into the butt of the gun and reached for an additional box of ammo. The box read: Hydra-shock, 100 rounds.

Normally, he didn't carry a gun while in the office or even out at public events. But because of everything going on over the last two days, he felt the need to carry it. It gave him a sense of importance. He had the respect of most of the people in Hope, but occasionally respect wasn't enough. This town understood guns and also understood the man with the gun had authority, regardless if he had a badge or not. Dunn had both, and come a standoff between him and some unruly local, he always won.

But this was something all together different. This was a death— another death he reminded himself—and anyone on the scene would want to know that someone of authority was in control. Death wasn't common in Hope, and the people would want to make sure their Sheriff could handle the situation, especially if it turned out to be murder.

32

Dunn stepped out of the cruiser and was met by Bill Shrader and a group of young boys on bikes. Dunn knew all of them and smiled as he walked up. "How are y'all doin' today, kids?" Dunn rubbed the head of the closest one, trying to look important and friendly all at the same time.

"Fine," the boys answered in unison.

"Bill," Dunn said, extending his hand.

"Sheriff, these boys are the ones who found the body," he said without any hesitation.

"I see. And how did that happen?"

"Well," the oldest one said pointing behind the hotel. "We found him up there."

Dunn knew him to be Robbie. He was about ten years old, short and fat with red hair and freckles. "What were you doing up there, Robbie."

"We were ridin' our bikes down Main, and Jeff here saw Tonka up by the trees sniffin' at somethin'. You know who Tonka is? That's Jason's dog."

"Yes, I know who Tonka is." Dunn thought of the numerous times he had to reprimand Jason for bringing that mutt in town without a leash. "So then what happen?"

Jeff spoke up, saying, "I hollered at the guys to stop and I ran up the hill to see what he was sniffin' at. I like Tonka"

"I see," Dunn said putting Jeff's fondness of the dog aside. "And what did you find?"

In a hushed tone Robbie said: "A dead guy."

"Okay boys, I want y'all to go on home and don't tell anyone about what you saw. Do you know what impeding an investigation means?"

"Yeah," Robbie said. "That's where you get in the way of the crime scene."

"That's right. And if I find out any one of you told so much as a bug I'm gonna arrest you and lock you up, understand?" Dunn didn't want to scare them, but before everyone in the town started asking questions he wanted some answers.

"Yes sir!"

The boys picked up their bikes and rode off, cutting through Country Cafe's parking lot. Dunn turned to Bill, who had waited patiently throughout the questioning, and laid a hand on his shoulder. "Now tell me what you saw." Bill nodded his head and pointed towards the woods.

They strolled through the hotel's parking lot and climbed the gradually sloping hill to the line of trees at the top of the short incline. A few feet into the woods Bill stopped and pointed at the ground. "This is what I saw," he said, indicating the half-eaten body of a black man.

The man's insides, or what was left of them, lay stretched out around the body. What looked to be his intestines extended ten to fifteen feet back into the forest. Probably an animal, Dunn thought. One of his legs had been torn off and was missing. A trail of blood led into the woods and past the length of the intestines. Dunn studied the face and tried to determine who it might be. All color had been drained from the face, but he could tell it was a black man by his facial features. He had seen dead black men before, but only in photographs, and those didn't match the sickening, ash-white color that was reality.

"Gruesome, ain't it?" Bill said, never taking his eyes off of the body. "I saw something like this in W.W.II. A guy in my unit got pinned down by enemy fire and a round got 'em in his gut. The round shot his guts out like that ten feet in front of 'em. Poor fella just kept on screaming that he wanted his mamma, all the while trying to stuff his guts back in."

"Uh-huh," Dunn said absently. He wasn't paying much attention to Bill as he studied the features of the dead man's face. There weren't many black men in Hope, but Dunn didn't rule out the possibility that this could be a drifter. He knelt down to get a closer look. Although the face had large chunks eaten out of it, Dunn thought he might know him.

"Whoever he was," Bill said, "he died scared."

Dunn nodded in agreement and bent down to grab the dead man's chin. His mouth hung wide open and he took note of the dental work. "He saw the dentist regularly. I doubt he was a drifter. He still has most of his teeth."

"You mean that may be someone we know?" Bill backed away, cupping his hand to his mouth. "Hell Sheriff. You don't think it's someone from around here, do you?"

"Yeah, I do. I know him, but I just can't put..." Then he had it. Dunn stood up and wiped his hands together. "That there is Earl Jackson. He works down at the school cleaning up. His wife cleans the Mayor's office. I'm sure of it."

"You don't say."

"Yeah, I do and Bill," Dunn looked at Bill for the first time since discovering the body. "What I said to those kids about keeping quiet goes for you, too."

"Oh, you don't have to worry about me, Sheriff. I won't say a word."

"Uh-huh. Let's see you don't. I want you to get me a blanket so we can cover him up, understand?"

"Sure, Sheriff, but I can't take any from the hotel. They cost money. I have to keep an inventory on them."

"Just do as I say, Bill."

Bill left, sliding down the grassy slope and Dunn watched him go. Two deaths in twenty-four hours, he thought. *I haven't even started with the accident last night and now I have a possible homicide. I'm gonna have to call Phil in early.* Dunn spotted his cruiser and heard the crackle of empty static coming from the radio. "I just hope he's got his radio turned on," he said aloud.

33

Jim Langley woke up late, still groggy from the night before. He had spent most of the night tossing and turning, marveling at the power Beliah possessed and the control over which he used it. He was so excited with the likelihood of meeting Beliah the next day at the bookstore that he couldn't sleep, and when he finally did the first rays of dawn were breaking through his bedroom window.

He set his alarm for 9:30 to give himself enough time to get dressed and run down to the book store right when it opened. That didn't happen, though. He never heard the buzzer, and at ten minutes to twelve he was barely able to register that he was late.

Jim rolled out of bed and headed to the bathroom, scratching himself through the hole in his boxer shorts. He had since given up opening the garage on Saturday's, due in part to the lack of business. Work, though, was the last thing on his mind as he relieved himself in the shit-stained toilet. Finished, he stuck his nose under his arm and took a whiff. Scrunching his nose in disgust, he reached for the deodorant and gave each pit a quick swipe before walking out the bathroom without flushing.

He picked up a pair of greasy work pants off the floor and slid into them. He made a quick search for a clean shirt, and finding none available settled for the matching work shirt that was hanging on the back of a chair. He groped the front pockets of his pants for his keys and slapped his rear pockets for his wallet. Finding both, he went into the kitchen/living room and plopped down on the only piece of furniture in the one bedroom rental: a green, bug-infested chair with hints of seventies nostalgia.

Jim stared with vacant eyes at nothing in particular. What little sleep he had the night before was filled with strange and horrible images of him watching a man being eaten alive. The dream itself didn't bother him all that much considering he has had bad dreams for most of his life. What did bother him was his dream-self enjoyed watching the beast devour the man, while at the same time wishing it was him doing the dining. He remembered waking up at one point with a hard-on.

He blinked, breaking his trance, dispelling the memory and slipped into his work boots. It was only when he stood up that he realized he had forgotten to put on socks. With a slight shrug he started out the front door and got into his beat-up, brown, stepside Chevy truck and fired up the motor. He sat for a few moments listening to the bellow of his beefed-up 350cid engine with its slight miss that only a car buff would interpret as a "Cam".

He put the gearshift into first and took off down the circular gravel road. Looping around, he stopped at the opposite side of the trailer park and looked both ways down Lee Street for any signs of traffic. On his left was a trailer slightly larger than his that belonged to Wanda Pritchard. He grabbed his crotch and thought, *One night I'm gonna get me some of that, Kevin or not.* Then speaking aloud he said. "Yes sir'ee bob. One of these nights, Miss Wanda, I'm going to tag that."

He gunned his motor, popped the clutch and pulled out of the park, the action shooting gravel at her bedroom window. He chirped the remaining three gears leaving twin sets of rubber at each shift point and floored it down Lee Street. Downshifting, he turned onto Main, saw the light green at the intersection and slammed the transmission back into third. The light hit yellow as he popped the clutch into forth and burned bright red as he made it half way through the intersection. He glanced in his rear view mirror and saw his garage on the right sitting dark and unproductive.

Looking forward, Jim almost ran down Sheriff Dunn, who was standing next to his cruiser in front of the hotel. The Sheriff had a roll of wide yellow tape in his hand and he threw it up into the air as he fell back into the cruiser to avoid being hit. Jim swerved into the oncoming lane, down shifting at the same time and popping the clutch once again. His truck quickly lost its forward momentum without him once applying the brakes. Jim prided himself on the ability to drive without braking.

He made a hard left into Lazenby's bookstore and glanced over his shoulder at the Sheriff. Dunn was standing in the center of the street shaking his head, his arms raised. Jim grinned to himself. By the look on Dunn's face, Dunn was going to let Jim get away with it. *It's going to be a great day,* he thought, and pulled into a parking spot. Lazenby came to the door to see what all the noise was about and gave Jim a friendly salute. "Is the book signin' still going on?"

"Yeah," Lazenby said, "What there is of it. Hasn't brought in as much business as I thought it would."

Jim gave Lazenby a black grin and got out of his truck. Climbing the stairs, he opened the door and stepped inside, looking around. On his left he noticed Beliah was signing a book for the red-haired boy that worked part-time at the hotel.

"You buyin' or looking," Lazenby said with some disgust.

"Oh, I'm buyin'," Jim said. "I like what this man has to say."

"You and a few others seem to be the only ones that do."

He ignored the remark and walked over to Beliah with his hand extended. "Hey Beliah, I heard you last night. I think you hit the nail on the head."

Beliah gripped his hand firmly and said, "I'm glad to hear it. You were one of those who spoke up last night, weren't you?"

Still holding Beliah's hand, Jim looked down, embarrassed and said, "Ah, yeah. I didn't know..."

"I like a man who speaks his mind, don't you?"

Jim looked up and his eyes locked onto the medallion around Beliah's neck. It seemed to glow in an ever-increasing pulse of purple light that extended outward. He tried to pull his hand away, but Beliah gripped it even harder. Jim's head was swimming and his world raced away from him. Beliah, and the desk with the stacks of unsigned books, rapidly fell away and all that was left was the glow of a bright lavender light. It gave him the illusion of looking through the wrong end of a telescope.

He was drawn into that light like being sucked through a straw. After a few moments of resisting, he gave in to whatever force was calling him. He flowed along splinters of light and felt himself moving faster and faster. The light surrounded him on all sides and had a strobe-like effect that caused him to lose all connection with his physical body. The medallion loomed in front of him, filling his vision. The words encircling the medallion grew to the size of buildings and then mountain ranges. He was swallowed up in their shadows.

His forward movement stopped and he had the sensation of falling, spiraling down into the center of the medallion and the sun embossed there. It looked like a molten furnace of dark yellow-orange flame. I'm about to die, he thought, and suddenly he stopped just inches away from the hot molten pit.

"Do you want to continue?" a dark, omnipotent voice asked.

He heard himself answering, "Yes," from somewhere above him, outside.

"Then here," the voice said.

Instantly, Jim was plunged into the lava, a searing pain engulfing him, obliterating him, liquefying his atoms. Then he had something in his hand and he lifted it up to see what it was. It was a book, Beliah's book.

"It won't blow up when you open it, you know," Beliah said smiling.

"What?" Jim looked up from the book to find himself standing in the middle of Lazenby's completely mystified. "What happened?"

"I just signed your book, man."

"Hey mister," it was the red-headed boy. "You look like death warmed over. You okay?"

"Ah… yeah, sure. T-T-T-Thanks Beliah. I'm gonna read it from cover to cover."

"Chill out, man. I didn't mean to scare you," Beliah said, and then in a hushed voice, "I didn't scare you, did I?"

"No," Jim said, trying to sound brazen and self-assured, returning Beliah's look with one of his own. "I like danger."

"Don't we all," said the redhead.

Jim looked at the redhead to give him a what-do-you-know look, but found the kid's expression filled with knowledge that maybe he did know something.

"Patrick knows all about it," Beliah said. "He got his book early, didn't you?"

"I sure did," redhead said, chuckling.

Jim nodded his head, acknowledging what was said and instantly his mind was filled with images of what really happened to Matt Richardson. He started to drool at the thought. "You do as I say," a voice in his head said, "and I will feed you." Jim thought back to his dream and smiled, understanding the full meaning of it, consciously aware of a warm throbbing in his pants.

34

He was still smiling a few minutes later when Wanda Pritchard came through the front door wearing a short denim skirt and a white sleeveless shirt. It was half-buttoned, revealing the fact that she wasn't wearing a bra. All eyes were on her as she scanned the faces of those in the store. She knew Lazenby, mainly because his store was across from the bar and they exchanged pleasantries. The red-headed boy she knew only by seeing him around town and she winked at him, causing him to blush slightly. Patrick, the redhead, had a crush on her and she knew it.

The only other two in the store were Jim Langley, from her trailer park, and the man from the bar last night. She went over to the table and casually glanced at Jim's crotch. "You happy to see me, or do book signings get you horny?"

Jim dropped his hands to his crotch and spun around, obviously embarrassed. Beliah laughed a smile and leaned back in the chair. "Wanda. So we meet again."

"Ah, yeah. Thanks for the tip. Now I can see why money's no problem for you. You're a big-time writer, huh?" She leaned forward, giving Beliah an eyeful, who took it indifferently.

"Money doesn't have to be a problem for anyone who reads my book. All you have to do is take control."

Wanda straightened up, a little disappointed at his reaction, but didn't show the slightest hint of it. "That's so," she said impatiently. "We've had other get-rich-quick gurus here before, but they're all the same. Buy their books or tapes or whatever and what you're left with is a pipe-dream with a hole in your wallet. So what's your scam?"

"I understand your cynicism, Wanda, but I'm not going to try to convince you of anything. I'm not going to make you promises I can't keep."

"Uh-huh. I guess I should count myself lucky you paid your bill last night. I should have expected you were a con artist." She gave him a final once over and twirled around, her hair flipping off her shoulders and settling on one side of her face. She went over to the counter and picked up a paper, slapping down a dollar bill. "I only came in here for the paper, Carl. I hope business picks up for ya."

"If it doesn't, it's no big loss. I don't do much business on Saturdays anyway. The paper is fifty cents, Wanda. Most people go to Montgomery or Birmingham on the weekends. This town's going to put me out of business."

"Yeah, if it wasn't for the drunks we'd have to shut Sandy's down. I'll see ya."

With that, Wanda left. When she reached the parking lot she looked over at Jim's truck and frowned. "That sonofvabitch broke my window," she said. "I'll teach him to spin rocks." She unfolded a small penknife and bent over next to his tire. "I can't," she said, "even though he deserves it."

She put the knife away and started across the street. Half way over, she stopped cold. Sheriff Dunn was parked in front of Sandy's with his head down, writing something. Cautiously, she moved in a direction away from the cruiser and closer to the bar at the same time. She made it to the door and was about to slide the key in the lock when Dunn spoke.

"Miss Pritchard, may I have a word with you?"

Here it comes, she thought, and dropped her hands, leaving the key hanging in the lock. "Sure Sheriff. What can I do for ya," she said, turning around and smiling the biggest and brightest and most innocent way she could.

"I need to talk with you concerning one of your customers last night. Can we go inside, please?"

"Sure. C'mon in. Can I get you something to drink?"

"Thanks, but I'm on duty."

Wanda unlocked the door and flicked on a single overhead light. "Hey, that's okay. I won't tell anyone. Phil comes..."

"Phil does what, Miss Pritchard?"

"C'mon, Sheriff, call me Wanda. Everyone does."

"Even Phil Hartman, my deputy?"

"Sure, whenever he comes in here." Wanda knew Phil had duty last night and that he was drinking his rum and cokes like a fish. She walked nervously over to the bar and passed behind it. She liked Phil and didn't want to get him into trouble, but she couldn't lie to the law. It was just one of those things with her.

"I didn't come to talk to you about Phil, Miss Pri...Wanda. I know he comes in here before duty some nights. And if he were to have a drink I would consider it a personal favor if you watered down his rum-n-cokes a little. No, the person I want to talk to you about is Earl Jackson. Know him?"

35

Jason finished his dinner and busted out of the house like a bolt of lightening, Tonka following close behind. His mind was running crazy with the images of a few short hours before. Who was Tamara, really? What was she talking about? Was Beliah as evil as she made him out to be? He sprinted down the gravel road leading away from his house and rounded Lee Street at full speed. Tonka bolted ahead, crossed Lee and made for the wooded path several yards down on the right. The path—the same taken Friday night—would bring them out behind the grocery store.

Dusk had fallen and a cool mist had settled over the paved road, giving it a slick sheen. Jason stopped running and breathed deeply, trying to catch his breath. Tonka had disappeared somewhere up ahead and Jason called out into the dank chill. "Tonka, here boy. C'mon boy." Jason's only response was his labored breathing echoing through the trees.

Suddenly, the machine-gun rattle of exhaust-restricted backpressure echoed wildly off of the trees and Jason looked in the direction of the noise. He saw the twin headlights of a large truck barreling down the road. The staccato ceased and was replaced by a crescendo of fuel-filled rage. There was only one vehicle in town that sounded like that. It must be Jim Langley.

The twin beams of light wove their way all over the road and Jason wondered if Jim was drunk. Backpressure followed by another blast of power gave Jason pause to wonder if maybe he should get off of the road, just in case the driver didn't see him. He moved as far as he could to the side of the road, facing the oncoming truck. To Jason's left, the shoulder was nonexistent and fell off sharply into a three-foot ditch. The truck moved closer.

Something about the way he was driving scared Jason. The truck was closer now and almost on top of him. He stopped walking and turned sideways, estimating the likelihood of reaching the other side before the truck would overtake him. He made to run across the road, then stopped. Tonka appeared out of the woods directly across the road and Jason yelled, "Stay, boy. Stay!"

The deafening bellow was all around him now and he turned to see the truck aiming right for him. What happened next was etched permanently in his mind, recorded in slow motion. Jason raised his arms across his face just as the front bumper passed close enough that the slack in his jeans slapped against his legs. The truck's side mirror caught one of his hands and spun him around. Jason tumbled away and landed, face first, in the ditch.

He was partially unconscious, but still lucid enough to hear the truck screeching to a halt. The driver threw the truck into reverse and backed up. Jason rolled over, feeling needles of pain shoot across his hand. The driver's face was illuminated in the green glow of the dash giving Jim Langley the look of a carnival clown. The light gave his contorted face a hideous, comical appearance. He climbed out of the truck and made his way around to the front. His silhouette, cut from the headlights, hovered over Jason.

"Hey boy," Jim spat. "Are you still alive?"

All Jason could do was moan.

Jim opened the passenger door, reached inside and removed a rifle from the gun rack above the seat. "Boy, you're going to pay for hittin' that mirror."

Jason managed to turn over into a sitting position, facing the truck. He stared in dumbfounded horror as the reality of the events sank in. Jason understood precisely what Jim was saying: He meant to hit Jason, hoping to kill him. Now, still alive, he was about to be on the receiving end of a shotgun. He clawed his way backwards into the ditch, ignoring the pain in his hand, trying to get away. A shot sounded and several small pellets kicked up dirt and grass only inches from his face.

"You don't think I'm going to let ya leave now, do you?" Jim chambered another round.

"H-H-H-Hey Jim, what's the matter, huh?"

"Beliah don't like you much, kid. No offense, but he wants you gone, see. He told me that if I took care of his problems, he'd take care of mine. Business ain't so good these day's, y'know?"

"But what—"

"Oh hush, son. I was hopin' to make it easy on you. You stood too damn close to the edge. I almost ran my truck into the ditch. I love my truck."

In spite of his fear, Jason understood that Jim Langley was more than a little nuts. There was no remorse, no sympathy. The man before him was nothing but a cold-blooded killer. "L-L-Look, maybe I could h-h-help you out, whadya say?"

Jim leveled the rifle at Jason, aiming right at his head. Pulling his face away from the stock of the rifle, he said, "Jason, there's nothing you or that bitch Wanda can do. Just live with it. Sorry, die with it." That last was followed with a blood-curdling chuckle.

Without a sound Tonka vaulted out of nowhere and came down on Jim's arm. The shot fired low, hitting Jason between his legs, and sent more dirt into his face. A six-inch section of Jim's arm above the wrist and below the elbow disappeared in the dog's massive mouth. Tonka bit down hard, showering his muzzle with blood.

Jim, out of pain and desperation, clubbed Tonka on the nose with the butt of the rifle. The dog fell to the ground, lost his footing and rolled into the ditch. Tonka quickly recovered and charged back up, launching himself at Jim. While in mid-air Jim locked Tonka in his sights, pulled the trigger and brought the dog down with a blast to the chest. Tonka fell dead at Jim's feet.

Jason screamed, "NO!" And then the rifle was aimed at him.

"I think you better sit back down, boy. I'm not through with you, or that mutt." He shifted the rifle under his injured arm and rummaged around in the bed of his truck. "There it is," he said, producing an axe.

With tears streaming down his face Jason whispered, "It's okay, boy. I'm here. It's going to be okay." Then with a heartbreaking scream, he hollered, "YOU BASTARD! I'LL KILL YOU!"

"Sure you will, boy. Right after I get through hacking up your puppy. Ever been to Korea? They eat dog there." Jim knelt down beside Tonka, lifted up his head by his ears, and placed the axe blade to his throat. "Ever eaten dog, boy?"

Jason watched with eyes wide in horror at what was about to happen. "No," he gasped.

"No? Let me cut you a slice." With that, Jim brought the blade up into the fleshy part of the dog's throat, stopping only when he hit bone. Then, welding the axe with one hand, he brought it down on the back of Tonka's neck, severing the head. He reached down and picked up the detached head by the ears. Holding it up over his head, he said, "I think I'm gonna have this one mounted. What do you think, boy?"

Jason rose slowly to his feet, seething. His fear and confusion had been replaced with hate. The anger that filled his insides burned with the intensity of a thousand suns. His eyes radiated heat and he stared directly at Jim's face. Jason felt energy welling up within him. Powered by the furnace of hate, an intense energy flowed out of his fingers, covering Jim in a fiery light of crimson.

Jim dropped the axe and threw his hands to his ears, pressing inward. "What's goin' on," he screamed.

"I'm goin' on, asshole," Jason hissed.

Immediately, Jim's head began to swell to gigantic proportions. A bloody-gray liquid oozed out of every orifice: His ears, nose, mouth and eyes. His facial features, grotesquely distorted due to the expansion, were stretched into a mask of horrible awareness. Just as the fluid discharge reached jet-like intensity, shooting high-pressured streams out of his eyes, his head exploded, covering Jason with a blistering mélange of muck and brain and blood the consistency of jelly.

Jason screamed.

The gooey mess oozed down Jason's face and arms and dripped off the ends of his fingers. He stood paralyzed with fear, wide-eyed in disbelief due more from the cause than effect. He raised a hand to his face, curiously sniffing the fluid collecting at the tips of his fingers. It had a rusty, wild, meaty smell, the kind Jason immediately associated with the liver his mother had fixed for dinner.

He doubled over, vomiting, spilling his guts in a torrent of yellow bile. Jason was close to hysteria and ran out of the ditch shrieking, waving his arms uncontrollably over his head. He had lost all sense of reason and was bordering on shock. His mind was closing in on him, shutting down. He couldn't cope with the reality of seeing his dog beheaded and then exploding a head just by thinking about it. Jason knew exactly what happened. He was about to slip into the final stage of denial and blackout when a small voice spoke to him.

"The first step in perceiving an alternate reality is to first accept its possible existence." It was the voice of the woman from his dreams, Tamara, but only the memory coming out of a dream.

He slowed his pace from a psychotic sprint to a rational stop in five short steps. Cautiously, he turned around and squinted at the headlights of the truck a hundred yards away. He went over the events starting from his first sight of the truck to where he was right now. He still couldn't believe he was the source of that power, but accepted the possibility of it happening.

"The mind is a powerful thing," he heard Tamara say. "It is capable of all sorts of accomplishments in the physical/ material world. Everything created, from the truck in front of you to the jets in the air, were once first an idea. Then, through physical manipulation, those ideas evolved into reality." Then a new thought began to form in his mind. It came together, clarifying his thoughts. It was beautiful and simple.

If technology is nothing more than applied thought and reality is nothing more than applied technology, then thought equals reality. Reality is whatever I believe it to be.

Jason started back to the truck thinking over this new insight. Is it possible, he thought, to control reality with just the power of your mind? The concept was too fantastic to believe but too potent to ignore. What had happened happened. That was the only sane thing his mind would accept. He had superheated the cranial fluids of a man simply by directing intense hate and anger on one spot.

He stopped walking and looked into the ditch. His dog lay a few feet away, dead. Tears spilled over his eyes and down his cheeks, blurring his vision. Wiping his eyes, his anguish turned to bitter loathing as his vision cleared and he saw Jim's body, his head splattered everywhere, also dead. "You son-of-a-bitch! I hope you rot in hell, bastard."

Reaching the truck, Jason leaned against it, swooning, emotionally drained, and discovered it was still running. "I've got to find Tamara," he said and then hopped in the truck. Grabbing a couple of oily rags that were sitting on the floorboard by his feet, he wiped his face and threw them in the back.

He had been driving for a couple of years and felt confident behind the wheel of most vehicles, but this monster vibrated with awesome power. Unnerved, he threw the truck into first and popped the clutch. He turned the wheel hard to the left and fishtailed around in the middle of the road.

It was close to ten o'clock when Jason turned onto Main, not sure where he was going. He passed the gun store and remembered the rifle Jim had used; it was still lying on the side of the road. He pulled up to the intersection and waited for the light to turn green. He looked to his right and saw Jim's garage, dark and rundown. Ignoring the light, he turned right, swung into the garage, and parked on the side. He killed the engine and stared at the church at the end of Commerce.

I can't go to the Sheriff, he thought, *not yet at least. What would I tell him? Hey Sheriff, I blew up Jim Langley with my mind after he killed my dog.*

Yeah, right. Pastor Blanchard was definitely out of the question. *He might believe I killed him with my mind, but he'd probably think I was possessed or something. I need Tamara, but how do I find her?*

Jason climbed out of the truck and ran across the street. He could just see Sandy's neon sign flickering at the end of Main. He shrugged and made for the bar hoping Tamara was a drinking woman. *Even if she's not there at least I can ask Wanda what's going on. Tamara mentioned something about her. Maybe she's like me.*

The thought was no more completed when he reached Sandy's. A sign posted on the door banned anyone under twenty-one from entering, but Jason thought he might be a good exception.

Slowly opening the door, he was instantly overwhelmed by blistering sound of distorted country music and the rancid smell of stale beer and cigarette smoke. The bar's interior was darker, in fact, than outside and he waited for his eyes to adjust to the diminished light.

"Sorry kid. You can't be in here," the woman behind the bar said.

Jason recognized her immediately as Wanda. Besides knowing she worked at the bar, and the fact that she was the only employee, Jason had a crush on her since shortly after losing his virginity. It was only last summer that he vowed to never sleep with anyone ever again until he made it with Wanda. It was many a night since then that he had imagined him and her together.

He started blushing heavily, lowered his head and shoved his hands deep in his pockets. "I'm looking for Tamara. I thought, you know, I might find her here."

"Look kid—it's Jason, isn't it? I don't know a Tamara." Wanda walked out from behind the bar and made her way to the door, flashing a sweet smile at him. Then gently putting her hand on his shoulder, she said, "You're gonna hav'ta leave. Dunn's been in here already today and I don't want to lose my license, okay?"

Jason was gushing and looked up to meet her eyes. They were brown, like a deer, soft and gentle, nothing at all like what he had imagined they'd be. His stomach felt queasy and his legs turned to rubber. He had never been this close to her, carrying on a conversation, smelling her.

"Jason," she said knowingly, "You gotta go. Maybe I can help you find this Tamara of yours when you're twenty-one, okay?"

"Sure, I—No, you don't understand. Tamara is a real person. I mean I think she is. I've seen her in my dreams and she told me that you and I were—"

"Yes, I'm sure you did. But look kid, I'm old enough to be your... older sister. Now go on." She pushed the door open and guided him outside.

"I know I'm not making sense, but you've gotta listen. Beliah is—"

"So that's the deal. Look Jason, that Beliah character is a scam artist. You do good to stay away from him and his books. This whole town is crazy over him; some good and some bad."

Then from inside the bar, "Hey Wanda, tell your boyfriend to scram. Kindergarten closes as soon as this place opens. I'm a payin' cust—"

"Oh shut your trap, Bill. You don't get room service here. Get you own beer." Then turning to Jason she said, "You just stay away from Beliah, hear?" She leaned over to kiss his cheek and the movement exposed a partially bare breast beneath her loose-fitting cotton button-down.

Jason's eyeful was cut short by the screech of tires directly behind them. Wanda pulled back before administering the kiss and Jason stumbled away, crestfallen at the missed opportunity. The tires belonged to a red pickup and in the truck an attractive, raven-haired woman sat in the driver's seat, looking at them.

"Tamara!"

"Tamara?"

Jason broke away from Wanda and bounced around in front of the truck. "Tamara, I've been looking for you. Somethin' has happened and I need to talk to you, bad."

"You're Tamara? The girl from Jason's dreams?" Wanda asked, astonished.

"And yours too, I would think."

"You've dreamed of her too, Wanda?"

"No! Just someone that looked like her, maybe."

"Come now, Wanda. I guess next you're going to tell me that you've never seen Beliah in your dreams either."

"Then it **was** him," Wanda whispered.

"Yeah, it's him. That darkness is his true nature. Get in Jason. I've seen your work. That's why I came looking for you. Wanda, trust your instincts. I'll be back after you close. He's almost ready to show himself. He has already set his traps. My advice is to close up early and wait for me. Lock the door and don't let anyone in. Anyone! Right now, the only people you can trust are Jason and me. Got it?"

"Yeah, but—"

"No time now, but I'll be back. Remember what I said. Jason, buckle up, we're out of here."

CHAPTER 7

We have so much faith in our science and our religion that we are blinded to our own self-worth. Each individual holds the key to the Universe. We have the answers to every question asked, but instead of looking within ourselves, we turn to science and religion with all of their dogmatic ideas. The key to the future lies within ourselves; answers that have been long forgotten; answers that are only now beginning to surface.
From The Book of Beliah
Verse 17

36

"YOU STINK," TAMARA SAID, TURNING her nose away from Jason.

"Gee, thanks." Jason blushed.

"Lighten up, kid. You've been through a lot in the last couple of hours. Did you think you would come out smelling like baby powder?"

Jason thought about that for a moment. Although a little embarrassed, he sniffed at himself. There was indeed a foul odor to him. It consisted of sweat and dirt mixed with a biting, pungent, acidic flavor, like the kind of smell you find in the plastic toilets scattered around outdoor rock concerts. It was the smell of fear and adrenalin, with vomit thrown in to give it that O' so special tang. And, oh yeah! We can't forget the blood and brains, some of which were still clinging to his hair.

"Here," she said, giving him a towel. "Wipe yourself down and take off that shirt. In the glove box you'll find a tee-shirt."

They drove in silence heading out of town. Jason pulled his shirt off and wiped himself down, especially under the arms. He ran a comb through his hair and it came back with gray-white meat trapped between the teeth. It looked like hamburger that had been left in the refrigerator too long. He fought back the urge to puke and tasted bile from an empty stomach. He started to cry.

"Hey, Jason. It's gonna be okay. You go ahead and cry all you want to."

"I ain't crying," he blubbered. "I just feel sick at what's been goin' on, that's all."

"I can understand that. I—"

"Hey, isn't that the Sheriff's car? What's he doing parked on the side of the road?"

"I don't think he is Jason. Look!" Tamara pointed to the left side of the road. A strong beam of light swung lazily back and forth across the ground, illuminating the ground and the occasional tree.

"There's another car down there," Jason noted as they rounded the curve. "It looks pretty banged up. You think—"

"So that's what it was."

"Yeah, it's another cruiser, I think."

"I'm not talking about the car, Jason. I'm talking about the... disturbance I felt.

The truck came to a halt at the end of Route Nine. Before them, stretching east to west was Route 22. A sign directly in front of them indicated that Alexander City was 62 miles east and Mitchell Lake was 5 miles west. Tamara checked the traffic—really unnecessary at that time of night—and turned left, following the signs to Mitchell Lake.

"Huh?" Jason gawked at her.

"There are a lot of things you don't know," she said. "Not yet. But I see you have grasped some of the truth."

"The truth of what, that I can kill with my mind?" Jason was still shaking over the events of the past few hours and his voice cracked several times.

"Truth lives in the eye of the beholder, Jason." Then pointing at him she said, "Truth is whatever you think it is. Understand?"

"I-I-I don't know."

Tamara swerved the truck off of Route 22 and down an unmarked gravel road. The turn was quite sudden and Jason felt the seatbelt tighten against him. The road, or lack of it, was lined with potholes and she did a great job of hitting every single one.

By the time she stopped, Jason's body, as well as his nerves, was badly shaken. "Ever think about driving in a monster truck pull? You'd win."

She put the truck in park and killed the motor. Backing up against her door, she faced him and said, "Thanks."

Jason didn't like the way she was looking at him. She was smiling, slowly moving her eyes over his body, sizing him up. Not once since he drove away with her did he bother to ask where they were going. Now, here he sat with a complete stranger in the middle of the woods, surrounded by trees on three sides and a large body of water in front. At any other time it would have been beautiful, something beyond his wildest dreams. Here he was with a gorgeous woman, in the dark, with—as far as he could tell—no reason for being out here but one.

She reached out with her right hand and just barely touched his cheek with her finger. He jerked away, frightened and horny. "W-W-What are we d-d-d-doin' here?"

Tamara busted up laughing. "Jason, I—oh boy—I'm not going to rape you, honey. It's just that I don't often get the chance to talk to—much less touch—such a soul as good as you. Where I'm from the physical can get you killed."

"So, where's that?"

"Are your parents going to get worried about you? I guess I should have asked you that before."

"Before I killed a man, you mean?" Jason's confusion over that had taken on a bitter expression. "No. They think Tonka's with me and—"

"You loved your dog."

"I just can't get it out of my mind how Jim could have done that. I mean I could understand him hittin' me and all. He didn't see me, you know. But when he got out of that truck, the... evil in his eyes—Tonka was only trying to save me. THAT MURDERING BASTARD!"

"You did to him exactly what he did to the thing you loved the most. You had no control over what happen. He determined his own destiny by his actions. It was those actions you focused on and... Did you really mean to blow his head up?"

"No. I just reacted, you know." Tamara nodded, and Jason thought she did know what he meant. "So what happened?"

"People like you and I—and Beliah for that matter—are mirrors of the things in the hearts and souls of those around us, whether that be good or bad. How we reflect that energy is determined by our own intentions. You are basically good, but untrained. Beliah is evil, pure and simple."

"I think I understand the mirror part, but does everybody have one?"

"It's not something you have, Jason. It's something you are and no, not everyone can reflect concentrated energy like us. You are born with it; it's something that can't be learned."

"But what about Beliah's book?"

"What about it?"

"It has a lot of stuff in it like what you are saying, but somehow I don't think it's the same. Is it?"

"You're very perceptive, Jason. What he has tried to do—not only here in Hope, but in other places and other times as well—is to sell the secrets to the non-gifted inferiors."

Jason was taken aback by the remark.

"Face it, Jason. You exist on a different plane of reality, the true reality. Your unconscious, or subconscious, is the only true reality. What you call consciousness is really a dream. All of this is a dream." She said, empathizing what she meant by slamming her fist down on the dash, driving her point home.

"If it is only a dream, then why is it solid?"

"It's only solid because you believe it is. The reality of this space around us now is held together by the combined belief of everyone who has ever come here. Right now, you are creating the illusion that this dashboard is real."

Jason gave her a confused, disoriented look, summing up how he has felt since the beginning of this whole mess. She smiled at his bewilderment, her full lips parting slightly, showing straight, white teeth. Jason had to hold back the overwhelming urge to kiss her.

"Let me back up sweetheart. You have an ability born to you that kings and sorcerers and wizards have tried to buy, beg, borrow, steal and like in the case of Beliah, kill for. He is evil and has always been evil. Our race—and I'm not talking about the human race—has existed for eons. We are eternal and immortal. Our purpose and where we come from is lost to history.

"Some claim that we are aliens from another dimension outside the known universe. That universe includes the reality of your dreams. They think we existed before this time in a kind of flux, an all-encompassing consciousness. We are sent here to serve, in a physical form, until events occur that bring out our abilities. Beliah's arrival in Hope is what triggered yours."

"So if I'm immortal, why can't I remember any past lives, or whatever you call them?"

"You do, in a way. Jason, until just recently you thought your dreams were... well, dreams. We don't have past lives to remember. For that matter, we don't have present or future lives either. We exist outside and beyond time. The concept of time in this reality is something mortal man invented to mark his progress. The human race took all of existence and narrowed it down to only one plane: Linear. The past will always come before the present and the future hasn't happened yet. That kind of thinking is wrong.

"Time is more like a ball than a line. Think about the latitude lines on a globe. All lines begin and end at the poles. There, a Traveler such as you can change lines and exist in a different point on those lines. This is a very simplistic analogy, but I think you get the idea."

Jason's head was reeling. So much information and he still didn't understand how he blew up Jim's head. All of this crap about time-traveling aliens. He didn't know what was real anymore and felt more frighten now than when witnessing Jim's incredible expanding head. He had so many questions to ask, but every answer Tamara gave raised a hundred more. He searched her deep, emerald-green eyes and smooth face for any sign of deception or trickery but only found the reassuring smile and look of deep wisdom. Whether he believed her or not, there was one thing he knew for certain: She believed what she was telling him.

Jason turned away from her and looked out across the lake. So calm and tranquil, the sight of it made him want to cry again. *Why did this have to happen to me?* He thought. When Sheriff Dunn finds Tonka and Jim Langley it won't matter if he is some kind of Traveler. The only place he would be going would be to prison, and probably for a long time. Jason had a momentary flash of him sitting in jail serving a life sentence, a beard reaching the floor and a calendar with the date Sept. 25. 2495. Three walls of his four-wall prison were covered with short chalk marks, four down and one across, repeatedly. He cringed.

Tamara took that cringe as continued confusion. "You don't have the slightest idea what I'm saying, do you? How long have you had your dreams?"

"I have always had bad dreams, but lately it's been every night or whenever I close my eyes. I guess they became regular about a year ago."

"Not that long, then. You have just reached the stage of separation without the exploration. Is that right?"

Jason nodded his head. "Yeah, I guess. Is that bad?"

Tamara frowned. "Well, it's not good. Normally, two of us don't meet in the physical/material, knowingly, until we've met in the spiritual."

"That's what we did, right?"

"Not exactly. You didn't meet me—I met you. I was following the path of Beliah when I ran into your essence, your soul. Obviously, you were in the beginning stages of realization. Whatever Beliah's plan is for this town, you weren't supposed to be involved. I must have mistaken your realization for your culmination. However, your ability is odd. There must be another reason our paths have crossed."

"So our meeting has nothing to do with Beliah?"

"We met because of Beliah, but that's not the purpose for your awareness at this time." Now it was Tamara's turn to look across the lake.

"Can I ask you a couple more questions?"

"Shoot," she said without turning away from the water.

"Who or what is Beliah?"

"Beliah is one of us, but a renegade. What little we do know about ourselves is that we aren't created evil or good. We are made one way or the other by the choices we make. Beliah's soul, his mirror, is clouded with hate. He distorts the energy of others and uses it for his own purpose. He has been around longer than anyone. At least I've never met or heard of anyone that was around before Beliah.

"Tradition has it that he either pissed off our Creator or got pissed off and refused to continue with his created purpose. Since his awareness, he has dedicated his life to his own twisted plan, one that puts him above all others as a god. At different times and on different levels he has succeeded. Human history is filled with his meddling."

"You mean he was like Hitler or something?"

"Hitler was one of his allies. Jason, I'm not talking about world domination. I'm talking about historical domination. Changing the course of past and future human events to where human time stops and all reality, in all of its levels, falls under his control. He thinks that he can become the Creator through his personal efforts. That is why Beings like us are here. I have trailed him across the world and across the Universe."

"Can't you stop him? I mean, you talk about changing reality with our thoughts and all, why can't you just get a couple of us together and—I don't know—blow him up."

"Jason, sweetheart, you have so much to learn. To do what you say would take more than three or four of us and the end result would be the total annihilation of the physical/material. And even then, he still wouldn't be stopped. There are always other realities."

Jason thought about that and then asked, "Then what's the point? The way you talk, he's all-powerful. I guess you're right. There's so much to learn."

"Yes, and now is not the time to learn it. Our time is running out. We must get out of here and find Wanda. She'll be waiting for us."

37

"I don't have a clue as to what you're talkin' about," Wanda said, eyeing Tamara suspiciously. "I have dreams, sure. Who doesn't? But that doesn't mean they're real or anything."

Tamara remained fixed on the road before her. Jason shot quick glances between the two women sitting on either side of him. After a few uncomfortable moments, he said, "Wanda, you better listen to her. She knows what she's talking about."

"I'm sure her little bedtime stories are fascinating, but I don't even know why I'm here. Look dream girl, you might be able to sell your fantasies to a boy, but I'm not buying it. If you don't mind, just turn this truck around and drop me off at my trailer."

Tamara slammed on the brakes, skidding to a halt in the middle of Route 22. "Look lady, I'm not here for my health," she said. "I'm trying to save your life. If you would just hear me out, I might be able to explain myself better. We're going to Mitchell Lake. That's where Jason and I just came from. It's safe there. Give me one hour. If you still think I'm nuts, then okay. Fair enough. I'll take you wherever you want. Deal?"

Tamara's hand shot out across Jason's chest and Wanda took it. "Deal," she said.

The brief connection between the two women produced a tingling vibration that ran up Wanda's arm and soften at the elbow. The strange jolt surprised Wanda and she released Tamara's hand too abruptly. Her arm below the elbow felt like it was asleep, like hitting her funny bone. Pins and needles ran up and down her arm causing it to take on a low intensity glow. Everyone in the cab of the truck took notice of her action but remained silent.

The feeling passed several moments later and then Wanda asked, "So what's this you say about the dreams being real?"

"Wanda, have you ever been in a cavern?" Tamara began.

"Yeah. I went to Carlsbad on my honeymoon."

"Your honeymoon?" Jason's jaw hit the floor.

"I'm not a virgin, kid. What did ya think? I never had a boyfriend or something?"

"No… I mean, I just thought you weren't the type to—"

"Jason," Wanda said, reaching up and stroking the top of his head, making him feel more like a puppy dog than a lover, "I'll take that as a compliment."

"So Jason, how does it feel to have a toe where a molar should be?" Tamara smiled at him and then at Wanda. The laughter was spontaneous and the tension between the two women vanished.

"So what about the caverns?" Wanda asked.

"Do you know what Helictites are?"

"It's a rock formation, I'm sure, but I couldn't tell you which one."

"You're right. They are the delicate, flowerlike formations that grow and hang from the ceiling of caves."

"Stalactites?" Jason asked.

"No, those are the cone shaped rocks that hang down," Wanda said. "I think I know which ones she's talking about. They develop in all sorts of directions."

"What?" Jason wondered what rocks had to do with creating with the mind. "Doesn't water drip down and spread out like pedals?"

"Not exactly," Tamara said. "They seem to defy gravity and grow sideways and also up."

"That's twice you've said grow," Wanda noted. "Are you saying that rocks are alive?"

"Yes! Geologists haven't a clue to what they are or how they can create formations such as they do, but I can tell you. You see, everything is alive.

Every tree, rock and even the clouds in the sky exhibit life. The simplest definition that I can come up with is this: To live is to create. And in the natural order of the Universe all things can create on some level. Even if that level is below, above, or beyond our understanding. It's that simple. It is through these forces of being alive that all things are made, and it is belief in these forces that unleashes the power to create life."

"It sounds like you are talking in a huge circle," Wanda said.

"Life is a circle. All things come into being through belief in the creation of life."

"What you just said sounds a lot like what's on that medallion around Beliah's neck," Jason said.

Tamara nodded her head, saying nothing.

"So I understand the words now," Jason said. "But what's the point of the medallion. And what's the deal about that crystal thing?"

"It's a doorway, Jason. The medallion is nothing more than a Talisman, a trinket to focus power. It's an attention-getter in order to lure you into his world and his way of thinking. The medallion has no power in itself. It is belief in its power that creates the force—draws the force would be a better word for it. The same could be said of any object. It acts as more of a catalyst than possessing any true power."

"Then it draws evil forces?"

"There's no such thing as evil forces," Tamara continued. "Think of an electric wire. Is the current running through it good or evil?"

"That depends on what it's used for," Jason answered.

"Ah!"

"I think I'm beginning to understand now," Wanda said. "But who are you and how do you fit in?"

Tamara looked across the lake and saw a dim glow rising in the east. The hour Wanda had given her slid away and was replaced by a second without any mention of it. "I am what most people would call a ghost. I only exist in the ethereal state. This body you see as Tamara is a product of my mind."

Up until that point Wanda allowed herself to be convinced. Most of what Tamara had said she could have found in any number of New Age books over at Lazenby's. But now, Tamara was telling her that she was a ghost and Wanda only thought she really saw her. She didn't buy it. "That's it. Now you're a ghost? And a ghost that drives, too. Give me a break."

"Wanda, what can I do to convince you that I am what I say I am?"

"Disappear!"

"Get out of the truck. You too, Jason."

"C'mon Tamara," Jason said. "It's a good ten miles back to town. Besides, I believe you. Don't blame me for what Wanda says."

"Forget it kid," Wanda said. "She's a fake. Probably works for Beliah. This act undoubtedly sells more books for him."

Tamara seemed impatient. "You asked me to disappear and that's what I intend to do. So please get out of the truck."

"You bitch. I didn't mean leave us stranded in the middle of the woods at night." Wanda opened the door, but didn't get out.

"This vehicle is a part of me," Tamara said, growing annoyed. "If I were to disappear like you asked with you connected to me in any way, I would pull the two of you with me into the spiritual. Jason would most likely be able to handle it, but you Wanda, couldn't. Not yet at least. Now get out. We don't have much time."

Jason and Wanda climbed out and walked a short distance away from the truck. Wanda leaned against a tree and Jason sat down, exhausted. "Well, kid. Either you and I walk all night and are the first ones at the cafe for breakfast or I'm checking into the nut house."

"Just watch, Wanda. Tamara's not a kook. I came to find her after something happened earlier. I still can't believe what happened."

"Remember what she said about believing, kid," Wanda teased. She wasn't about to accept the testimony of an impressionable boy. She looked down at Jason, who was staring glassy-eyed at the truck. Either somethin's up, she thought, or that Tamara chick has him by the balls. A maternal feeling (or was it jealousy?) gripped her. She fought it down and then asked, "Did she screw you?"

"What?"

38

Tamara cleared her mind of all material thoughts and entered an altered state of mind, one lacking boundaries and infinite in space. It was devoid of light, but darkness wouldn't be the word she would use to describe it. The human physical/material mind couldn't handle the concept of a place without light but apart from dark. The idea is contrary to the absolutes that humans give to everything. They believe there is a gray between right and wrong, good and bad, but refuse to acknowledge that those concepts are two opposing ends of the same spectrum. Their form of rationalization is the gray in between.

Tamara knew extremely well the paradox of their belief system and the fact that it couldn't hold on to that which couldn't be measured. Unfortunately for them she also knew it was the unseen that was the true measure for the seen.

These thoughts drifted in and out of her mind/space, forming pictures instead of words. Words and numbers had no place in this realm. They were solely used in the dominion of the physical/material. Humans created them in a feeble attempt at communications. It was ironic, she thought, that man's greatest achievement, the computer, was nothing more than a means of communication. The pinnacle of their collective lives was the storing and passing on of information. A task that the spiritual world took for granted.

If there was anything Tamara needed in the way of information—and information wasn't necessarily knowledge—she could open her mind to receive the impressions of the life forces around her. Buildings, trees, anything that was in the center of daily activity could serve as a recorder for information. Humans, however, weren't aware of this fact and so built objects to house their gathered information.

Tamara felt a tremendous vibration and the non-light, non-dark of her mind filled with the absorbing brightness of her Being. The illumination began in the center as a point and expanded in magnitude until she became nothing and everything, fully embraced in the reality of the spirit. She was neither alive nor dead, but a part of the overall creation of the master plan for the Universe.

39

"Nothing," Wanda said. "It's none of my business what... Jason, look!"

Jason followed Wanda's trembling, pointing finger and saw a bright, shimmering light envelope the truck and its driver, partially obscuring Tamara within it. The light had an intense, milky luminescence that frayed at the edge, producing a silhouette of the truck. The contrast to the night gave Jason the impression of something out of a sci-fi movie, or his dreams, real and yet artificial. The image lasted for a few moments and then vanished, taking with it both the truck and Tamara. Jason stood up and shoved his hands deep into his pockets. Wanda gawked in disbelief and bewilderment, unable to speak. Even Jason's movement went unnoticed by her.

Jason broke the silence by speaking first. "I guess you owe her an apology, huh?"

"Y-Y-Yeah, I guess I do. Where the hell did she go?" Then in a whisper, "Where did she go?"

Then a sound, like the thunder of a jet passing over, penetrated the vacancy left by the missing truck and that same milky light reappeared. But this time, instead of the outline of a truck, it was a car. The light winked out and Tamara reappeared sitting behind the wheel of an older, 70's Camaro.

"What do you think of the new wheels?" she asked through the opened passenger's window.

Noticing Wanda still had a problem speaking Jason took on the most obvious question. "What happened to the truck?"

"I didn't want Wanda to think that what happened was merely an illusion. Besides, Beliah knows what I was driving. No sense tipping him or his cronies off to our presence. Get in. It'll be dawn before we get back to town. I'm sure he'll have everything ready by then."

40

Wanda had seen many things in her twenty-five years of life, but nothing to compare with the sights and ideas of the last few hours. She sat quietly in the front of the Camaro, staring out at the growing dawn. Tamara was going back to town, driving like a woman possessed. A thought formed in Wanda's mind that maybe Tamara was crazy. And maybe she was as well. She looked around the interior of the Camaro and noticed it was immaculate. The black cloth seats were in perfect condition and matched the short pile carpet under her feet. Even that looked like it was recently vacuumed. The only dirt visible was what she brought in on the soles of her shoes.

The lack of dirt and filth she associated with cars of this age focused her mind on other items that were missing. The dash had a plastic cover where the radio should have been, and upon a quick inspection of the glove box and console she found nothing, not the first scrape of paper or even a speck of dust.

"You won't find anything," Tamara said without taking her eyes off the road. "I don't create anything I don't need. Waste of energy."

"Not even dust?" Wanda asked incredulously.

"If I don't think dust, I don't get dust. You understand that Jason?"

"Yeah. It makes sense," he said. Then, "Why did we have to go out of town to talk? Seems like a big waste of time to me."

"Beliah knows we're here. He already tried to kill you once in the physical and several times in the spiritual. We needed a place outside of his perception. And in this case, anywhere away from town is it."

"So Beliah has limits?" Wanda asked.

"We all have limits, but I don't think that's what you mean. Beliah is only concerned with your town at the moment. In the spiritual, he can come and go as he pleases, but trying to find us in the physical would take more energy than he would want to use. That doesn't mean he won't have his disciples looking for us. He knows we won't sleep until he is gone or destroyed, so searching for us in the spiritual is out."

"What do you mean, 'won't sleep'?" Jason asked.

"Jason, the last time you fell asleep he almost had you. And would have, but for some reason he held back. He wants you, probably for the same reason why you're here now."

"Because he thinks I'm hunting him down? I didn't even know about him until this morning... yesterday, whatever."

"Jason, you have a power that you don't understand and I'm not talking about just the ability to reflect energy. Your whole development has been different from the beginning; yours too, Wanda."

"Huh?" Wanda was half-listening to the exchange between them, more out of disconnected confusion than anything else. All the talk about power and reflections merely bounced off her without being fully absorbed. "Are you trying to tell me that I have the same power you have? Give me a break, lady. I can't even balance my checkbook."

"No surprise there. Most of us have a feel for numbers, but not a full understanding. The greatest mathematicians in the world are as dead as doorknobs, nothing inside. They don't have the ability to express any concept outside of known reality. You see, those that are forced to live their life in the physical/material will always have to speak of it in terms that cannot be expressed any other way, and those terms are limiting. Words, as well as numbers, limit the truth to just those concepts. Nothing else can exist beyond those concepts."

"What you mean," Jason concluded, "is that in order to see the spiritual, you have to believe in its existence."

"You, my friend, are learning."

"Oh my God," Wanda said, pointing down Main street. "What happened?"

CHAPTER 8

For most people, every thought or feeling is based on this material reality.
From The Book of Beliah
Verse 12

41

SHERIFF DUNN RECOILED FROM THE sight of the severed hand lying on the underside of the wrecked cruiser. The light from his flashlight gave the mangled appendage an appalling yellow glow, turning the blood almost green in color. He drew closer to it, and picking up a twig he poked it wondering if it would move on its own. It didn't. He searched the interior of the cruiser for any evidence of what could have happened to cause the severing of Phil's hand and found nothing. Blood was broadcast in a concentric circle around the car giving Dunn the impression that Phil was searching for something either in the car or near by.

He heard the crackling of twigs coming from just inside the tree-line and aimed his light in that general direction. The beam caught the reflected retinas of three large animals staring back at him. Slowly removing his pistol from its holster, he hoped he wouldn't have to use it.

The wild dogs, however, only gave him a cautionary glance and then went back to their business of digging in the ground, devouring something.

Dunn felt panic suddenly rise from the pit of his stomach as he realized that the meal the animals were clearly enjoying might be Phil. He darted up the embankment to his car, slipping on the dew-covered grass, and yanked the door open. He grabbed the shotgun out of its carriage and skidded back down the grassy incline.

"Phil!"

The dogs stopped eating and moved a couple of feet away, never taking their eyes off of Dunn. He moved in closer to the tree-line and the dogs began circling themselves. Dunn wondered if they were deciding whether to stay and fight for their meal or run. He hoped the latter, but raised the shotgun to his shoulder anyway and continued moving forward.

Three steps into the woods Dunn swore he could hear his heart pounding, driving the barrel of the shotgun up and down with every beat. On the fourth step he kicked something hard and metallic. Tearing his eyes away from the dogs for a moment, he looked down, squinting in the dark trying to see what he had kicked. Simultaneously, his brain registered a shovel at his feet and the fact that one of the dogs—the largest one—broke into a sprint towards him and was now airborne.

Dunn's instincts screamed at him to crouch down, ducking beneath the animal, but it was too late. He did manage to cover his face with his forearm, but that just gave the dog a firm target to latch on to. Feeling the excruciating pain of the bone-crushing bite, Dunn cried out, fell backwards, allowing the full weight of the dog to land square on his chest. I'm about to die, he thought.

The pain in his arm gave him a moment to note what his other arm was doing and he realized it was still wrapped around the shotgun. He twitched his finger and the thing went off, just inches from his leg. The dog that had landed on top of him jumped off, terrified by the blast. Dunn took the opportunity and rolled to his knees. The other dogs stood a submissive distance back observing the larger dog's reaction. It was holding one of its hind legs slightly off of the ground. Its head was lowered, presumably weighing its options.

"C'mon dog. Show me your teeth so I can blow them out." Dunn's arm was throbbing, making it hard to hold his weapon level.

The dog set its back leg down and tensed its haunches, preparing to leap. Dunn inhaled deeply, easing the pain in his arm, and let it out half way. The dog jumped, and Dunn fired off a shell. The shot covered the dog's underside with several small holes, each one oozing blood. The animal landed in a heap at Dunn's feet and inhaled twice before it stopped breathing.

The other two dogs fled at the second shot, leaving Dunn with the trophy of a dead dog and the remains of whatever they were defending. He wrapped his injured arm with a handkerchief and pulled it tight with his teeth. The rising sun splashed yellow light across a mound of freshly laid dirt. A bloody stump of a foot protruded a few inches out of the mound. The ankle was small, larger than a child's but smaller than a man's. Dunn kicked some of the moist dirt away and noticed the leg was clean-shaven, obviously belonging to a woman. "Phil, what have you done?"

He dropped to his knees and began digging, scooping the fresh dirt out with his hands. Shortly, he uncovered the blanket-wrapped head of: "Angie Harris! Oh my God, Phil. My God."

He fell backwards and scrambled away from the body, making for his car. He slipped behind the wheel and keyed the ignition. He was in a near panic. He reached for the 2-way radio, putting the microphone to his lips, and then set it back down. "I've got to get to town. Find the Doc."

He shifted the column into drive and punched the accelerator. Within minutes, he was turning the corner to Main and almost drove into the tail-end of a Camaro parked in the middle of the street. Locking up his brakes, Dunn skidded to the right of the Camaro before coming to a complete halt. Getting out of the cruiser, he shouted, "What the hell is this?"

42

"Daddy?"

"Yes sweetie," Carl Lazenby said, sitting behind a pile of books in his back office. It was just after six in the morning and he had come in early before church with his daughter to finish up the books from the day before. He was in a fair mood because Beliah had brought in several people from out of town just to buy his book. Yesterday started out lousy, but before he could close down late last night he had to run off the few remaining customers thinking they would never leave. He was grateful to Beliah for the best one-day's profit since he opened.

"Do you like Tommy?" His daughter asked.

He set his pencil down and studied his daughter's face. "Sure, I like him."

Leaning forward across his desk, Missy said, "I mean, do you really like him?"

Lazenby noticed his daughter didn't have on a bra and frowned disapprovingly. "I said yes. What's the point?"

"The point is daddy," she said, now sitting on a stack of papers. "I made love to him."

Lazenby gawked at the remark his seventeen-year-old daughter just made. His astonishment promptly turned to anger and he rose out of his seat. "Why are you telling me this?"

"Because," she said, now sprawling across the desk on her back. "We did it right here on your desk. I thought you might want to hear it from me, first."

"What?"

She sat up, swinging her legs around to his side of the desk, spilling everything to the floor. Missy spread her legs wide on either side of her father, resting her feet on the arms of his chair. Her knee length Sunday dress rode up to mid-thigh, revealing an obvious lack of modesty.

Lazenby pushed his chair away, banging it into the back wall. He didn't recognize his little girl anymore.

"But he wasn't the first, daaaaddy. Wanna know who was?"

He shook his head, comprehending at once that the girl before him wasn't his daughter. He knew, intuitively, that some... thing had taken his daughter and replaced her with the morally obscene slut before him.

"It was Beliah. Tommy was nothing but a toy to give me pleasure. It's Beliah that I want. I'm leaving with him today."

"Enough!" He shouted, knocking the chair away. "You're not going anywhere but over my knee." Grabbing her by the arms, he pulled her off the desk and slammed her up against the wall.

"Daddy? You're hurting me." Her voice was soft, almost pouting.

Lazenby saw for the last time the eyes of his daughter, his real daughter. He loosened his hold on her and forgot everything that had just taken place. "Sweetheart, I'm sorry. I—"

Missy kneed him in the groin and then said, "Do him, Tommy. Kill the bastard."

Tommy poked his head around the door holding a large caliber pistol at his side. His face held a blank expression and it reminded Lazenby of his days in Boot Camp and the thousand-mile stare the recruits learned to exhibit. "Do him," Missy hissed.

Tommy raised the pistol and pulled back on the hammer.

"Kill the Bastard."

"Tommy, wait," Carl Lazenby pleaded. "You heard what she said about you. You mean nothing to her. It's Beliah she wants."

"Shut up, daddy. Beliah says you've gotta go. No loose ends. Tommy knows that he either comes with us or stays. If he stays, he's as good as dead. Tommy!"

"Tommy, think about what you're doing. Don't—"

The deafening report drowned out Missy's high-pitched giggling. The round hit Lazenby in the face, throwing him against the wall, upsetting the chair again and finally bringing it down on top of him. Tommy was trembling all over, still holding the gun out in front of him. Missy bounced over to him and threw her arms around his neck.

"Thank you, lover," she whispered.

"Missy? What have I done?" He was sobbing.

"You did just what I wanted. C'mon, let's get out of here. Beliah will want to know that you passed. He said he didn't know if you would, but I said I'd make sure you did."

Tommy lowered the pistol and studied the fallen figure behind the desk. Dark red blood, the consistency of corn syrup, flowed easily from the hole in the middle of Lazenby's face. His nose had been obliterated, pulling his eyes inward, forever looking into that of the other. Tommy gave a discerning thought to whether Lazenby saw himself the moment before the round ripped off the back of his skull. He didn't think Lazenby had. "Too quick," he said.

"What's too quick, love pole?"

"He didn't see himself," he said flatly, emotionless. Tommy stuffed the pistol in the front of his jeans, the barrel still warm, and pulled his sweat-shirt over it. He inhaled, sampling the aroma of the room. A pungent sulfur odor filled his nostrils, and like hearing a familiar song his mind drew back to the night before last in his father's store.

Tears welled up in his eyes, blurring his vision. The loss of his father stung and the depth of the pain surprised him considering he felt nothing for Lazenby. The sudden realization of his father's death swallowed the horrible reality of what he had done. His mind called out to him for vengeance. Why not take the life of another? Tit for tat, right?

Missy stood at his side, grinding her hips into his leg like a dog in heat. Her hands ran over his body, stroking the barrel of the pistol through his jeans as if it were a sex organ. He found no physical pleasure in her sexual gyrations—he was impotent now—but allowed her the indulgence.

"Whadya say, shaft? Right here, right now?"

A small voice gasped within him, an echo of a dying conscience. "This is perversion, Tommy. Don't." And then it was gone, replaced by another, more fervent voice. "Was it not perversion to take your father? Was it not perversion that caused her to sleep with Beliah?"

He went for the body, pushing Missy aside and peered over the desk. "I'll show you perversion," he said, chuckling. Removing the pistol from his pants, he unloaded three more rounds into Lazenby's skull.

Missy panted in the corner, groping herself. "Oh, Tommy," she cooed.

"Let's get out of here, bitch. Beliah needs us." Tommy started for the office door, snatching Missy by the hand as he went. He inserted the pistol back into the waistband his pants, feeling the warm barrel against his skin. Although still physically impotent, the heat aroused him. A song by the Beatles danced in his head, the same line repeating itself as if stuck in a loop.

"Happiness is a warm gun, bang, bang, shooooey." Yes, he thought, it is.

43

"Now those definitely were shots," Wanda said, looking in the direction of the bookstore.

"Yeah, they were," Dunn agreed. Then, "I want all of you to take cover behind the cars and don't move until I say so."

"I'm going with you," said Tamara matter-of-factly.

"Lady, I don't know who you are, but the answer is no. Wanda, you're in charge."

Dunn rushed across the street and fell against the wall. He reached for the Glock and peered around the corner expecting whoever fired the shots to come out of the front. He swung back around facing the two cars sitting on Main and observed the small group totally ignoring what he had said. He nudged the brim of his smokey-bear hat back with the barrel of his gun. Sweat poured down from his exposed hairline. A sound, like a note played on a child's xylophone, rang out. It was the welcome bell hanging over Lazenby's door. *It's amazing*, he thought. *I must have heard that a thousand times, but thought nothing of it. Now, it might mean the death of whoever is in there, or me.*

Holding the barrel of the pistol to his chin, Dunn counted to three and jumped out from behind the wall. "Hold it right there."

"Sheriff!" Missy said, startled.

"Missy, wha—Who's in there with you?"

"Just me and Tommy. We were cleaning up after yesterday."

Still keeping her between the cross-hairs, Dunn shouted, "Tommy, come on out. Now!"

Tommy stepped out and stood next to Missy on the steps. The two of them looked about as natural as two teenagers who had got caught in the back seat of daddy's car. They shifted around nervously and, except for the shots, Dunn thought that maybe he did catch them using "Daddy's store" for business other than selling books.

"Who fired the shots?"

"What shots, Sheriff?" Missy batted her beautiful brown eyes at him and stepped off the steps onto the cement sidewalk.

"Stop where you are, Missy. Where's your father?"

"Why, he's in the store. You wanna come in and see him?"

Tommy snickered and then said, "Yeah, he's just laying around. Go talk to him. He's got a real open mind right now."

Both of them busted up laughing and Dunn noticed Tommy lowering his hand to his gut. "Tommy, put your hands down to your side. I think the two of you need to come over here nice and slow."

"Tommy?"

The voice came from behind and Dunn shouted over his shoulder at the approaching boy. "Jason, get back. Now!"

"Tommy? What are you doing?"

Dunn caught out of the corner of his eye the gleaming barrel of a gun being pulled on him. He dropped to his knees and rolled away a moment before Tommy fired. The round hit Jason in his shoulder and the impact shoved him back, knocking his feet out from under him.

Dunn rolled to his left, coming up on one knee, and fixed Tommy in his sights. "Tommy!"

Tommy wheeled around to face Dunn and fired two desperate shots over Dunn's head. The brick wall behind Dunn exploded, showering him with chunks of broken crimson rock. Dunn returned fire and created a cavity the size of a golf ball in Tommy's chest. Missy ran past Dunn screaming, heading for the gap between the post office and the Sheriff station. He charged after her, and after a short foot race caught up with her, tackling her to the ground. She let out a sharp cry as he landed squarely on top, burying her face in the parking lot.

"Take it easy, Missy. Don't make me shoot you, too."

"Father!"

"Don't worry, I'll call your—"

"Beliah. Father. Unholy father. Beliah. Help me!" Missy bucked and twisted under him, trying to throw Dunn off. He wrestled against her, realizing that the tiny figure beneath him was stronger than her 105 pounds should have been.

44

Blanchard got up early Sunday, dressed in his familiar coat and tie, and after telling his wife goodbye he went to church. He unlocked the solid oak front doors and stepped inside. The temperature inside was a little chilly from the A/C running all night and he propped the doors open to allow the growing warmth of the day to filter in. The doors opened into a small narthex with two tables on either side holding a visitor sign-in on one and two collection plates on the other. He passed both without a second glance and walked through the nave passing several aisles and stopped before the altar.

The altar was built in three section; two sections before each row of seats and a third in front of the central aisle. Behind the altar were the chancel and the pulpit from which later this morning he would preach. He stared at the pulpit, terrified. Not since he was a young man had he felt the fear he now had. It was the fear of being at a loss of what to say. Already this weekend there had been two deaths, and according to what Sheriff Dunn had said both were labeled as possible homicides.

He knelt down, eyes fixed on the large gilded cross, and wept. Somehow, somewhere, he had lost his faith and the events of the last two days intensified his grief. He tried praying, but nothing came. An evil had gripped his soul, keeping his conviction bound like a man tied to a tree. He had a momentary vision of himself being burned at the stake: fingers of flame licked up his legs consuming all that it touched. He shook the vision away and opened his eyes. The cross blurred through his tear-filled eyes and then vanished completely, only to reappear after blinking several times.

"I hear you're in need of a secretary, Father."

Blanchard turned around, startled by the intrusion, and slowly stood. "Phil? What in God's good name has happen to you?"

"I had a little accident. Nothing too bad, but I'd be damned this hurts." He held his left arm up for inspection.

"Phil?" Blanchard started to approach him. At first he was apprehensive and then, moving closer, horrified.

Phil Hartman appeared to be totally unaware of his condition, at least from a sane point of view. Blood mixed with mud and sweat covered his brown deputy uniform. He stood in the doorway like something out of a cheap horror movie with his severed stump of an arm stretched in the air and his other one down at his side, working the grip of his pistol nervously.

"P-P-Phil, have you seen Doc—"

"I don't give a rat's ass about no doctor. I've come for the secretary's job. Have you filled it?"

"Phil, Angie is my secretary. She has been for several years."

"Well, I've got news for you, brother. She ain't gonna show up for work. She kinda had an accident."

"My God! Was she with you? Do you want to sit down and tell me what happen?" Blanchard eased slightly, thinking if Phil and Angie had been in a terrible accident that would explain his condition and maybe his interest in her job. He didn't understand, though, why Phil thought it necessary to come to church before reporting it to the Sheriff.

"You just don't get it, do you preacher man. I killed her. I beat her to death. At first I didn't think I did, but Beliah assured me that I did. She was a slut. I used to screw her every chance I got. In fact, we did it right there on the altar you were kneeling next to. We left the mess for your altar boy to clean up."

There was nothing for Blanchard to say. He backed away from Phil, closing one hand tightly around the cross that hung from his neck. He stumbled backward against the altar and landed hard on his tail-bone. An intense, searing pain raced up his spine and ended at the base of his skull, throbbing like a jackhammer.

"It's time to pay the piper, Marky. Philly likes willies. Do you have a willy or do you have to cut it off when you become a preacher?" Phil cocked his head to one side, conveying a sense of complete calm and sincerity.

"That will be enough, Phil," said a deep voice from behind them.

Phil moved out of the way and Blanchard stared directly in the eyes of Beliah.

"But Beliah, my lord, I was just—"

"Now, now, Philly. If you are good I will let you have that nice boy down at the hotel."

"Patrick? Yeah, Patrick." Phil bounded over to Beliah and crouched down behind him, like an animal, rubbing his head against Beliah's leg."

Blanchard said, "Beliah! Now I know where I've heard that name before. Beliah... Belial. That's the name of the Devil."

"At your service," Beliah said, bowing. "Or should I say, you're at my service?"

"How dare you come in here? This is the house of the Lord."

"Ah, but it was the house of your lord," he hissed. "The moment you lost your faith the power of your lord left. Now all that is left is an ordinary building dedicated to a dead man."

"No, that's not true. The Lord—"

"Your lord is nothing. All he ever was, was the combined belief of the worthless people you call your congregation. Without you as their focus their religion disappears like dew in the morning."

Still gripping the cross, Blanchard pulled down on the chain, breaking it and held the cross up before him. His hand trembled visibly. "The Lord will never leave me."

"Ha! What do you think I am—a vampire? All you hold in your hand is a meaningless piece of stamped steel. It wouldn't even be worth the trouble to melt it down. So put it away and join me. Come, you have already taken the first step. Hand me that cross and together we can rule this town." Beliah held out his hand.

"I-I will never join you, you spawn of Hell." Blanchard prayed he sounded confident, but felt himself being pulled to Beliah like a river coursing towards a waterfall. He quietly prayed for his soul to be taken before his human weaknesses drove him into a pack with the devil. A moment later, he was still alive.

"Come now. Surely you still don't believe that God exists? That belief was for your ancestors. To be truly human you must let go of that belief. Come to me, my child. Let go of that yoke of slavery, it is nothing more that a prison religion. Come to me and I will tell you about the truth of existence."

Blanchard started forward, stiff legged like something out of a Frankenstein movie. The parody made Phil laugh with a chilling howl that broke his resistance. Blanchard walked trance-like over to Beliah, his mind giving in to the Black Hand that had a lock on his soul.

"You see, Philly? Even a man of God has no power over me. I am truly God and there is no other."

"Yes, father. My lord."

"Leave us, Philly. I need you to find our enemy and report back to me." Then, speaking to Blanchard, he said, "In the meantime, we will get to know each other better. You will give me your soul and I will give you knowledge—just a small bite out of the fruit from the tree."

Phil bolted out of the church howling, obviously insane.

Blanchard watched him leave and tears streamed down his face. He knew that once he reached Beliah he would become just like that, unable to even comprehend his own existence. He would become a slave to the blackness of his own soul; the evil that he knew was always there.

"You shouldn't cry, preacher. What you don't know won't hurt you. Besides, that which you see in Phil is that which lives in all humans. He is indeed his own captive. The only difference is that instead of living for this reality, he—as well as you—will live for me. It won't be so bad. I will just release the demons that are already within you. And just like Phil you will think you are happy. Imagine, never again will you have to search for the answers, for I will give them to you. Instead of worshiping your god, you will worship me."

"No," Blanchard whispered. He was now only a foot away.

"Silence, slave. That is a warning. The next outburst and I will remove your throat."

Blanchard's resolve was gone. He handed the cross to Beliah and instantly felt vanquished, depraved, damned. He felt a buzzing sensation rise in the pit of his stomach, filling his chest, flowing down his arms and out the fingertips. He teetered, seesawing on the heels and balls of his feet, and surrendered the only life he had ever known. He dropped his hands to his side and found himself barren, inhabited only with the memories of a past life that now seemed to fade like the visions of sleep. He felt suicidal and fell to his knees.

In front of him to the right was the table with the collection plates. He used them every Sunday, not only to collect money, but more importantly to collect faith. He preached the doctrine of sowing and reaping before each offering and knew the money collected was an example of the faith of his flock. It was more than just tithing —it was an exercise of belief in God to return it to them thirty, sixty, and a hundred fold. Now the plates lay empty, like his soul. Who would come to exercise belief in him?

"On your feet you worthless example of piety. You can't even hold on to your own soul. You're a waste of an embryo. From this day forward you will grovel at my feet, thanking me for sparing your petty, bankrupt life. Do you hear me?"

Blanchard, standing up as order said, "Yes sir."

"Lord, you imbecile. I am your lord. And I said you will grovel at my feet. Now grovel." Beliah backhanded him to the floor.

Blanchard proceeded to kiss his feet, saying "Yes lord. Yes master. Thank you lord for saving my life."

"That's better. Now look at this and I will show you the future."

Beliah unbuttoned his flannel-cotton shirt half way and revealed the round medallion hanging powerfully on his chest.

Blanchard stopped kissing his feet and stared at the crystal in the center. It emitted a dazzling beam of flickering light like that of a flame. The effect gave him tunnel vision, a sensation like looking through a paper towel tube, aware of nothing but the crystal. His mind fought against the flood of black light coming from the medallion, entering through his eyes, searing his mind and conscience. His last rational thought was that of his wife saying, "Mark, did you hear? Angie had sex with Phil Hartman on the altar."

"Doris, how in the world do you know that?"

45

Beliah smiled quietly to himself: He was quite please. *Soon this town would fall like the others,* he thought, *and in a matter of days the people would become like Blanchard.* Beliah kicked him in the crotch, breaking the connection between Blanchard and the medallion.

"You've had enough training. It is time to go and assemble the others. That bitch Tamara must be destroyed before she ruins my plans. Come!"

Beliah went out the door and Blanchard followed close behind. It was close to nine o'clock and soon the Sunday school crowd would be pulling in. The fountain was still off from the night before and they had a clear view of City Hall. There wasn't a car in sight.

"What do you say, preacher? By the time—"

The sound of gunshots echoed through the quiet city streets. Beliah closed his eyes and focused on the sound. He reached out with his mind and searched the morning air, allowing his consciousness to roam the streets and minds of the material world. "Ah. So the fight began without me. We must go to Lazenby's." Silently, he commanded his disciples to gather at the bookstore.

"I will expect you there within two minutes," he told Blanchard, then winked out of existence.

46

Blanchard picked himself up and nodded obediently. His thoughts, although cloudy, still exhibited some minor independence. He was able to contemplate his condition, but had no control over his emotions. He found that pain and pleasure had somehow mixed, becoming the opposite of what his mind told him they should be. The kick in the groin was an immediate example of this modified orientation. His body throbbed in pain, but his mind registered extreme pleasure. He mentally restrained himself from asking Beliah to kick him again.

This must be how a drug addict feels, he thought, knowing full well that the thing you most want will hurt you and may even kill you. He squeezed his crotch harshly, kneading his swollen testicles. Renewed pain filled his gut and he suppressed the desire to smile.

As the pain in his testicles subsided, Blanchard became aware that Beliah had disappeared. Panicking, Blanchard raced around the building to the parking lot. His mind fought against itself over whether to run through the woods and cross Main between the bar and the print shop, or drive. Given his age the sanest decision would be to drive, but he smiled at the thought of his heart exploding in his chest. What pleasure that would bring! He laughed wildly at the thought and darted across the parking lot heading for the woods.

Less than five minutes later he came out of the woods barely noticing the blood and bits of flesh laying on the ground that just yesterday belonged to Earl. His heel came down on a small puddle of that mess and his foot slipped out from under him. He came down hard but still he continued laughing. The fall broke his arm, and a bone from the compound fracture jutted out just below his elbow. He tweaked the bone and became ecstatic with the painful sensation. On his feet again Blanchard continued his race to beat the clock, his arm dangling out from his body.

He passed between the bar and print shop and stopped on the sidewalk, breathing heavily. Across the street he saw several people. Two were kneeling around a fallen boy and another was putting a handcuffed girl in the police car. A third lay, presumably dead, by the door of Lazenby's. *I guess he won't be coming to church today,* Blanchard thought. Beliah was nowhere to be seen. Looking around nervously like a lost child, He was becoming frantic, thinking that he was late and Beliah had left without him. He called out to the group, almost shrieking. "Has Beliah been here? Where's Beliah? Have you seen him? What have you done to him?"

Dunn was the first to respond. "My God, Pastor! What happened to you?"

"God had nothing to do with this," he giggled, and then he raised his broken arm. The portion of arm below the elbow peeled away from the bone and hung down. The palm of his injured hand twitched uncontrollably.

Wanda screamed.

"I'll kill you," Blanchard said, starting across the street. "I'll kill you all." And then, locking eyes with Tamara, he fell to his knees, weeping. "Please help me."

"Shoot him, Sheriff," Tamara ordered. "For his own good, shoot him."

"I-I-I can't shoot him. Pastor Blanchard?" From somewhere deep within him Blanchard found what remained of his soul. He realized what Tamara was and her presence had released him temporarily of his bondage. "Please son, kill me. I have sinned before God. This may be my only chance. Shoot Me!" And then he started clucking like a chicken.

"Sheriff, either you do it or I will," Wanda shouted. "I know things seem crazy, but there's a reason."

Dunn leveled the Glock at Blanchard's head, but couldn't pull the trigger. "I can't. That man baptized my son. I just can't."

"Then I will."

Dunn's pistol flew from his hand as if jerked away and landed in Tamara's opened hand.

"Wha...?"

Tamara unloaded one round into the middle of Blanchard's head, blowing out a hole in the back of his head. Blanchard staggered for a moment and then fell to the ground, dead.

"Things are getting too crazy around here," Dunn said. "I'm gonna need answers right now or I'm locking you up for murder one. Now hand me that pistol, nice and slow."

Tamara flipped the pistol over, catching it by the barrel. "Here. It's Beliah."

"Dammit to hell. What's all this about Beliah?"

"I think I can explain, Sheriff," Jason said, sitting up.

"Son, I thought you were unconscious. How's the arm?"

"That's one of the things I want to explain." Then turning to Tamara Jason said, "I healed myself. I understand now."

"I was hoping you would," she said.

"Healed yourself?" Dunn looked like a boy who just learned there wasn't a Santa Claus.

"Yeah," Jason confirmed. "I left my body right when I got hit. I didn't even feel the bullet. I saw everything that happened after that. I saw you shoot Tommy and then tackle Missy in the alley. I saw how she fought. She almost got away."

"How could you know that?"

"I told you… I left my body, and while Pastor Blanchard was screaming at you I healed my body. Of course, I'm not too sure how I did it. I just thought about it. Does that make sense, Tamara?"

"Yes, it does. You have crossed over without the help of a guide. You have truly become a Traveler."

Dunn was starting to lose his cool, not able to process what was happening. "Can anyone explain to me what is happening here without leaving their body to do it?"

47

Jason quickly recounted the events of the past few days and how they related to Beliah's appearance. He told Dunn about Beliah's true nature and his ultimate goal of world domination.

"You mean to tell me," Dunn said, shaking his head vigorously from side to side. "That sweet little Missy is a spawn of Satan? I can't believe that. No way."

"Sheriff," Jason said. "Little Missy would have killed you if she had the chance. And what about Tommy? Not only did he try to shoot you, he shot me. He might have killed me."

Dunn nodded.

"Speaking of Tommy," Tamara said. "Don't you think it's time to see who he shot?"

"You're right." Dunn glanced at his cruiser. Even from thirty feet away he could see Missy screaming and kicking in the back of the cruiser, perspiration dripping down her face, matting her hair. He had never seen, or really believed, anybody could be possessed, only pictures in comic books and Hollywood movies. However, watching her from a distance, he started to wonder if there really was something to what Blanchard said every Sunday.

"Wanda," Dunn said. "I want you to come with me. I may need a witness."

"Sure Sheriff."

"Jason, you sure your arm's okay?"

"Yeah Sheriff; I'm fine. But I can save you the trouble of going in there. I've seen it. It's not pretty."

Still uncertain over Jason's and Tamara's claims, Dunn gave them a shrug and said, "How 'bout we exchange notes when we get back, okay? C'mon Wanda."

The two of them entered the bookstore and Dunn once again took the pistol out of his holster. Checking the side of the magazine, he counted the small holes that ran the length of it. Every fifth hole had a number corresponding to the number of holes and therefore the number of rounds. Dunn counted four missing from the twenty-round clip.

"Sheriff?"

"What is it Wanda."

"Why did you really want me to come along? What gives?"

Dunn put his index finger to his mouth in a gesture for silence. They ventured past the checkout counter and made their way down a row of books. An open box lay butted up against the backside of the row and Dunn casually glanced inside. There were maybe twenty books set binder up inside. He read the title: WITCHCRAFT: A STUDY INTO THE MYTH by Beliah. No last name! He stopped at the far end and held up his hand, giving indication for Wanda to wait. He proceeded through the back and paused by the door leading to the office. The palms of his hands were wet with perspiration and his gun hand had a slight twitch. He took a deep breath and opened the door. "Son-of-a-bitch!"

"Sheriff, you okay?" Wanda asked as she peered around the corner.

"Yeah, but don't come in here. It's a... mess. I thought I told you not to come in here."

"Too late. My God! Did that boy do that?"

"It's only circumstantial, but yeah, I think he did." Distraught and shocked about the events of the last few days, Dunn fell back against the wall, exhausted, the brim of his hat bent flat against it. He pulled it off and nervously played with the brim. "Do you believe what Tamara and Jason are saying?"

"Is that why you wanted me to follow you into the store?"

"Yes."

"I don't know what to believe. I don't remember most of my dreams, but I remember some. It's those dreams I wish I could forget. They scare the daylights out of me."

Looking up from the ghoulish mess around him, Dunn glanced at Wanda and nodded his head. "Can you tell me about them?"

"There's not much to tell, 'cept that I've seen Tamara and Beliah in them. Now I'm pretty open-minded to most things and I would even bet that maybe I had some premonition concerning him and her, but the other stuff... I don't know."

Dunn nodded. "If they would've told me that stuff two days ago, I would have suggested they spend the weekend down at Meadhaven. But all that has happened—and Pastor Blanchard? What they said makes some sense. But the devil, in the flesh, here in Hope? Wanda, don't repeat this to anyone, but I think Phil's gone over the edge, too. I found his car on Route Nine. Anyway, I discovered a body near the accident. It was Angie Harris. She had been beaten to death and buried in a shallow grave. Some dogs had gotten to her. I think Phil did it."

"Phil? I know he's had some trouble lately, but do you really think he could have done that?" Wanda asked, surprised.

"I guess I don't have to tell you that he's been seeing Angie. Don't look so shocked. He told me about it. Besides, it's not a big town."

Wanda nodded. "Yeah, I knew he was seeing her and... well, I might as well tell you. He would get drunk over at Sandy's before duty and then meet her in the back lot. From what he told me she liked it rough. Say, do you think that maybe it was an accident? Maybe they were doing something weird and she died?"

"Maybe, but I saw the body. She was brutally beaten to death. If that was her idea of foreplay, I wouldn't want to see their version of sex."

"What did you find out about Earl?"

Dunn's eyes grew big. *Yesterday*, he thought. *That was only yesterday.* "In light of what has happened lately, it would suggest Beliah. He was the last one seen with him... what, Friday night? And Matt Richardson. I wonder if his death is tied into all of this. Do you know how Beliah determines who he kills and who he doesn't? I mean, you and Jason seem to be on the good side while Phil, Missy, Tommy, and Blanchard are on the wrong side. How is the decision made?"

"I'm not too sure. Tamara would know, but I think it has something to do with faith and belief. If you have a strong sense of values I guess he can't get you. Tamara says it's all done in the, ah... dream state. He controls their minds by controlling their dreams or something like that."

Dunn checked his watch. It read: 9:48. The town was too quiet. Everyone he knew either went to church or opened for business at ten o'clock. The streets should be busy with traffic, especially in front of the cafe. That was the normal meeting place for everyone, either getting breakfast or not. Something just wasn't right. He glanced once more at the body of Carl Lazenby. "That makes four murders and one fatal shooting in less than three days. I'm never gonna be able to explain this to the Mayor. She's—"

"Dead boss," Phil said from the doorway to the back office. "Just like you're gonna be unless you join with the master."

"Phil, what are you doing? Put that shotgun down. That's an order." Dunn studied Phil carefully. Phil had a shotgun draped over his wounded arm, fingering the trigger with his other. He looked deathly ill although diseased would have been a better word for it. His injured arm had a green color to it up to the elbow and splotchy, pale-white circles covered most of his face and neck. He looked feverish. His dead eyes showed no recognition or life whatsoever, and his color was like that of a corpse.

"I don't take orders from you, Sheriff," Phil said. "Throw your gun down and move. I think it's time for you to meet your future."

Dunn laid the Glock down on the desk without a word and went out of the office, keeping Wanda between him and Phil. *Phil's crazy*, he thought. *Not just crazy because he killed Angie, but crazy insane.*

Then Dunn had an idea. "Looks like your master couldn't sell out."

"What?"

Dunn pushed Wanda forward and out of the way, confident she would know what he was up to. He reared back with his elbow and tried to knock the shotgun out of Phil's hand. Instead, Phil pulled the trigger at the same time and fired into a row of books, blowing them to shreds, sending fragments of paper and binding drifting around the room. Grabbing the barrel and jerking it with all of his strength, Dunn tore it out of Phil's hand and sent it flying across the floor. Phil staggered back and scrambled towards the office.

"Phil, stop!" Dunn shouted, and then to Wanda, "Get out of here. This is gonna get bloody."

Phil reached for the revolver Dunn had left on the desk and whirled back around firing.

Dunn jumped behind another row of books and knocked them over, causing a domino effect with the few remaining rows. Working himself out of the fallen-over shelving, Dunn saw the shotgun laying a few feet away. He thought about going for it, but took cover behind the jumble of books and shelving instead.

"Give it up, Phil," he roared, eye-balling the shotgun. "I'll blow a hole in you the size of Montana."

Ignoring Dunn, Phil squeezed the trigger and set off a barrage of bullets.

Books and shelving exploded around Dunn, absorbing most but not all of the rounds. Two made it through. One skinned across his cheek and another ripped through his shoulder. He screamed in pain at the impact. A couple more rounds were fired and then, nothing. The Glock had run dry.

Phil threw the pistol at him and charged, screaming. "Ahhhhh!"

Dunn had a moment to determine his fate. He dove for the shotgun that was laying just within reach, adrenaline coursing through his veins. He snatched up the weapon and placed the butt in his shoulder with only a moment to spare. In that moment, Dunn locked eyes with Phil and pulled the trigger. It was a gut shot at point blank range. Phil was lifted off of the floor by the force of the shot and fell back, landing, ironically, on top of

Beliah's books. His body twitched as if experiencing a seizure which, Dunn thought, he probably was.

Dunn pulled himself up, wincing at the pain in his shoulder and stepped across the scattered books towards Phil. He knelt down and saw the sheer terror and pain in his eyes. The twitching had stopped and Dunn reached out to him, compassionately, placing two fingers on Phil's neck. There was still a pulse and he said, "Phil, don't die on me. I'm sorry partner. You left me no choice."

"I'll show you choice, you bastard." Phil reached up and put a vice-like hold on Dunn's crotch.

Dunn fell away, gasping, almost blinded by the pain.

Phil sat up with a jerk and clamped down tighter, giving it a hard, painful wrench. "You can't kill me. Beliah said I would live forever."

Dunn, with his eyes squeezed shut from the pain, lifted the shotgun up and hoped it was pointed in the right direction. He fired and the blast took half of Phil's head off. Phil released his hold and Dunn rolled away. He didn't know what hurt more, his cheek, shoulder, or groin. He rested for a moment on his back with one hand on the trigger and the other on his crotch. "I'm sorry, Phil," he whispered. "I'm really sorry."

48

"Get up, Sheriff. The master's waiting for you."

Dunn opened his eyes and saw a young, severely bruised girl pointing an AR15 assault rifle at him. "Missy? Where'd you... Never mind. Beliah's out there, isn't he?"

"Yeah and he's got your friends, too. You shouldn't have killed Phil like that. Beliah will be upset."

She backed away and Dunn got painfully to his feet. She made her way to the front door, walking backwards, never taking her eyes off him. She stepped outside and he followed her. The sun was above the height of the surrounding buildings and the glare blinded him for a moment.

"Nice of you to join us, Sheriff," Beliah said. "We've been waiting. I see you've taken care of a couple of my disciples. Did they die honorably?"

"He came right after we went in," Wanda said. "When I came out I was attacked by Bill Schrader. He's got him, too."

Dunn scanned the scene hastily and noted the location of the "bad guys". Missy was right behind him with a rifle shoved in his back. Tommy, still dead, lay at the foot of the steps. Bill Schrader stood over by the Post Office wall pointing a large caliber pistol at the base of Wanda's skull. Patrick, the red-headed boy, sat on Dunn's cruiser with another AR15. Beliah stood in the street off to one side of Jason and Tamara, smiling.

"We can't move, Sheriff," Jason said, making a good guess to his first question.

Tamara said, "It's an energy field. He took us by surprise. All of what has happened here in the past hour was designed to keep us busy."

Dunn rotated his shoulder several times trying to get the stiffness out. His wound ached, but it appeared the round went in and out. "An energy field? Now I've heard everything."

"Allow me to explain," Beliah said. "In this reality energy is released, not created. Just as a runner will burn energy through his efforts, he will also release unused energy at the same time. His body will try to keep him from over heating and thus thermal energy flows freely from his body. It is that energy, along with countless other sources, that I can harvest without much effort.

"I store energy with this." He pointed to the medallion that hung from his neck. "I can also store the energy of humans. Your Pastor Blanchard would have called that energy his soul. I can take this energy, and through the force of my belief, create whatever I please. In this case, that creation becomes a self-sustaining field. They are my captives." Beliah smiled pretentiously.

"Is that true, Tamara?" Dunn asked.

"Yes. Our own body heat supports the field. The more we struggle, the stronger it gets."

"That sounds like something from Star Trek."

"Maybe," Tamara said. "Only this is based on the laws of thermal dynamics. The field is generated using waste energy and supported by its very nature. It's an energy-absorbing creation. It's the opposite of a mirror. Just by me talking makes the field stronger."

"Yes, yes, yes," Beliah said. "All this talk bores me. Sheriff, I suggest you sit down on the step and keep poor Tommy company. Missy, come here!" The last was given as an order to which she carried out immediately.

"What do you want, Beliah?" Dunn winced as he sat down, his groin still throbbing with pain.

"What I want, human, is for you to die. There is nothing you can do for me except that. After all, you did take the life of several of my disciples. And look at Missy. She's been heart-broken ever since her lover was gunned down."

Dunn saw a look of contempt in Missy's eyes. She aimed the rifle at him and then smiled brightly. It gave her face an almost angelic appearance despite the bruises. She really was a beautiful young woman and Dunn knew that she would kill him the instant Beliah ordered her to.

"Just so there won't be any more trouble Sheriff, I want you to witness my power in this reality. Patrick, come here."

The red-headed boy jumped off the cruiser and sprinted over to Beliah. He stared at him affectionately, like a little boy might look at his father, hoping for a pat on the head. He was proud to be called by Beliah.

"Is your rifle loaded?" Beliah asked him quietly.

He's gonna kill him, Dunn thought.

"Yes master."

"I don't believe you."

Patrick took on the look of a hurt little boy. He pouted slightly at having his word doubted. "I'll show you, father."

"Great idea. Stick the barrel in your mouth and pull the trigger."

"No!" Wanda screamed.

Patrick rejoiced at the opportunity to prove himself and bit down on the barrel, swallowing the flash repressor. A second later Patrick pulled the trigger and fell to the ground. The back of his skull had blown off and bits of brain decorated the windshield of Dunn's cruiser.

"Now, are there any questions?"

CHAPTER 9

*If everything has meaning, then we cannot know the meaning of
anything until we know the meaning of everything, for nothing
exists in a vacuum. This cannot be done through normal reasoning.
Therefore, we know nothing until we can see beyond the normal.*
From *The Book of Beliah*
Verse 22

49

"NO!" WANDA SCREAMED. "YOU BASTARD."

"You son-of-a-bitch." Dunn said, spitting out the words. "If I get—"

[Jason! Can you hear me?]

"my hands—"

Out of the corner of his eye Jason observed Tamara calmly watching the grotesque scene unfolding before them. The scene was blurred because of the distorting intensity of the surrounding field. Did she say something? He found out shortly after being restrained that the more he moved the stronger the field became. It fed off of them, sucking them of energy, using that energy. Even talking became a chore. After speaking to the others a few minutes ago, the field had decreased in volume and was now completely encasing them like a glove.

[Jason! It's me, Tamara.]

"on you—"

That wasn't a sound—it came from within him, like in his travels. At what point did he stop thinking of them as dreams and begin regarding them as a form of travel? Tamara was speaking directly to him, mind to mind. Was this a form of telepathy? He shouted out with his mind. Tamara, I can hear you! Then nothing. Again, softer, Tamara?

[Jason, you're trying too hard. I can feel you speaking, but can't make out what you are saying.]

"I'm gonna—"

Feel me? Jason thought about that for a moment and realized that feeling was exactly what he heard from Tamara. He closed his eyes and thought of the warmth he felt as she spoke to him. He remembered the times she had appeared in his travels. There was always incredible warmth associated with her. He thought of the buzzing sensation and realized that only when she was around did he feel that warmth. Beliah always brought cold.

It was in that instant Jason understood the major difference between Tamara and Beliah. *So that's how he determines who his victims will be.* Jason thought of warmth and a vision formed in his mind of two lovers meeting. The lovers were faceless entities wrapped around each other in an embrace of love and security. He merged with one of the entities and immediately felt the buzzing sensation.

Whether he was in his body or out of body he didn't know. What he did know was that he felt warm and safe. Now he understood why Tamara could watch that horror beyond the field and not flinch. He called out to her with his mind, [Tamara.] This time there was a connection and the other entity became Tamara.

[Jason, I was beginning to think you wouldn't find your way here.]

[Is this the way Beings like us communicate?]

[Every Being has their particular... signature. Most are very abrupt with no ethereal contact. They communicate with word pictures, like we have done before.]

Embarrassed, Jason pulled away and distanced himself from Tamara. His essence took on a cloudy, rose color. [I'm sorry, I didn't know... I just thought that was the way it was done.]

Tamara moved in closer, once again connecting with his ethereal form and said, [Jason, I didn't say I minded. I'm enjoying this. It has been a long time since I have joined with someone in this way.]

Warmth flooded him, filling him with serenity and peace of spirit. [But I'm too young—]

[There is no such thing as time in this reality, Jason. I am as old or as young as you perceive me. We are, in truth, timeless.]

The two forms moved freely around and through each other: at one point two distinct Beings, and at another, one. They exchanged memories and lives together. Wrapped within each other, Jason saw the events of the last three days through her eyes. He felt what she felt; he knew what she knew. He wondered how long they had been in this state and suddenly, before the thought had completed, he knew the answer as Tamara thought it. [There is no time here. We are in a form of stasis with the rest of the world.]

[We can control time, then?]

[No. Time still exist for them and continues to move forward. However, we have separated ourselves from that linear time-frame. To return you would need to desire a union with it, either in physical or spiritual form.]

[I still don't understand.]

Jason felt Tamara smile. It was more of a sweet feeling than a compassionate one.

[You understand the physical, and I agree the spiritual is more complex. What you would call ghosts exist in the linear time-frame. They experience the slow passing of time without any means of escaping it.]

[Truly that would be hell.] Jason only meant to think that to himself, but of course…

[In a sense, that's what it is for those lost souls. It sounds like a cliché, but that's what they are.]

[They're what Tommy and Missy will become, right?]

Tamara didn't think anything and Jason knew he wasn't right. He felt pity pouring from her and he wanted to know why. He transferred his thought into her thought, his mind into her mind. And there, deep within her, was the answer. She echoed the thought back to him.

[They're completely gone, Jason. Their life force was totally drained away. That's what that medallion does. They lost their soul. When their bodies died, there wasn't anything left to move on. Their essence is no more.]

[But energy can't be destroyed. It can only change forms.] He was raised Christian and had strong beliefs about the afterlife, especially now after all he had learned. The state he was presently in only reinforced that belief.

[You're right, but the form they might have taken may very well be in the stuff Beliah used to form this energy field. I'm sorry.]

[What do we do now?]

[Escape. I can't, but you can.]

[Escape, how? And why can't you?]

[Who I am in the physical is an illusion. Tamara the woman doesn't exist. Just like in the woods last night with the truck turning into the car. I maintain my physical shape by thinking about it. If I choose to remain in the physical I can't leave from this space. Even now I am sustaining my body in the physical at a considerable drain on my available energy. That field is sucking me dry. You, on the other hand, are still very much physically orientated. You can escape and leave your body behind. It will appear like you fell asleep standing up.]

[But why can't you just disappear and then reappear outside of the field?]

[Jason!]

The feeling Jason received was one of impatience.

[I can't do anything in the physical without first manipulating the spiritual. Beliah won't follow me into the spiritual and he knows I can't harm him in the physical. He exists beyond both realms. He's the next step beyond us.]

Jason let that thought sink in. Up until then he believed that maybe, with the combined power of Tamara, Wanda and himself, they could defeat Beliah. After the word pictures Tamara sent and their desperate meaning, Jason knew they didn't have a chance.

[What can I do?] Jason asked pathetically.

[Good. He won't notice you gone. Although we sustain the field, Beliah uses his medallion to create it. You must remove it from around his neck. Without direct contact to it, everything and everyone under his influence will be released. It will only be for a moment, but that's all it will take to break the field. Once the connection is broken, he will immediately take control. We'll only have a few moments.]

[Can't I just take it away and hide it?]

[Jason, his power isn't in the medallion. He has real power. The medallion is more of a transmitting devise. It allows him to do other things without concerning himself with unimportant things. And right now, we're unimportant.]

[How do I remove it if I am in the spiritual?]

[You must use Missy.]

[What?]

[The body we call Missy is just a shell. Just like our field, the medallion controls her. You must take the place the medallion has in her life and tell her to remove it. Quickly.]

Jason was getting upset. [You want me to possess her. Tamara—]

[Not possess her. You might get stranded within her body if Beliah catches on to what you are doing. Speak to her in the spirit. The mirror that was her soul still exists within her, although it's more of a broken window now. Reflect your thoughts off of it and she will respond.]

[Reflect? How—]

[You'll know, Jason. Now go, return to physical time and do as I say.]

Jason felt Tamara pulling away from him, a kind of melting. The feeling left him cold and abandoned. She had returned to the physical and now it was his turn. However, he had to remain in spirit when he did. He open his mind and thought of his body; it felt like it might have been a million miles away. He felt a slight buzzing sensation and then the world, the physical world, flooded his senses.

He felt drunk and not fully in control of his body. He perceived the world through an enhanced state. Sights, sounds, and even the pressure of the field weighed heavily on him. The feeling lasted only a moment and then he realized he wasn't in his body, but riding it. He could see everything that was happening around him, but knew his eyes were closed.

"kill you, whatever you are!"

"Oh my, Sheriff. Do you really think you can hurt me?" Beliah said laughing.

Tamara was right. Jason found himself back at the same time as when he left.

"Why did you have to do that?" Wanda shouted, struggling against Bill Schrader's hold.

Jason turned to her and saw his vision swim away, then steady. His head hadn't move, and now he discovered he was looking out of the side of his head. His spiritual mouth was where his physical ear should have been. He knew he was wasting time and thought himself out of his body. He rose several feet in the air and observed the scene from above. He drifted over to Beliah and Missy and then thought himself down. Beliah was saying something to Wanda, but he only heard it distantly. While in this state he could only hear with his physical ears. And judging by the expression on his body's face, he was sound asleep. Whatever was being said, it came through like a dream.

He floated between Beliah and Missy and studied her face. She looked like a Barbie doll. Her eyes were glazed over and had no sign of intelligence within them. She had the AR15 rifle pointed directly at Dunn and her finger was resting on the trigger. Jason had no doubt that if Beliah as much as twitched his nose she would open fire on the Sheriff.

Jason thought at her, trying to make some sort of contact. Missy didn't respond and he tried again. Nothing. *I haven't the slightest idea what I'm doing*, he thought. Spiritually, he put his hands on his hips. Seeing movement over Missy's shoulder, he noticed his body reacting to his thoughts. His physical arms twitched at his sides, rising a few inches before falling back.

Great. That's just what I'm trying to do with her. Then he remembered what Tamara said. She had told him that Missy was like a broken window now. His thoughts had been directed through her and realized in his own physical body. He would have to "reflect" his thoughts. That meant coming in at an angle. But how was he supposed to do that?

Instead of thinking at her, Jason thought about her. He pictured in his mind the times he had seen her with Tommy. The image was sharp and painful. A heavy tear seeped out of the corner of his physical eye, spilling down the cheek on his physical face. He pictured her in the bookstore, seductive and voluptuous, rubbing her body against Tommy.

The picture cracked and he saw the same scene from a different angle. He saw it through her eyes. Her memory, he realized, was vivid, and through her he remembered Missy looking lustfully at Beliah. He felt the memory of her rotating her hips against Tommy's crotch. It had been Beliah. He had taken her virginity as well as her soul. Tommy never had a chance. The picture widened, disengaging from the remembered scene in the bookstore, and was replaced by the present. He had made contact. He saw everything from her point of view. He thought about the rifle and mentally slid his finger off of the trigger. She did the same. He briefly considered the possibility of turning the rifle on Beliah, but then decided against it. He glanced sideways at Beliah, catching a glimpse of the medallion half in/half out of his shirt. He could see it and so could Missy.

She was staring at Beliah and Beliah asked, "Does this bore you?"

Jason became aware that he could hear. Beliah's voice must have triggered that. He will expect an answer, but not too smart of one.

"No, my master," Jason said through her.

"That's my girl. After I'm through with this town, you and I will celebrate."

Jason was overcome by a fuzzy, lustful feeling low in her abdomen. No, lower. Her body was excreting hormones in response to Beliah's comment. Feelings, he thought. Even without a soul, this body had feelings. Without a soul the human body is nothing but a carnal, sensuous object. He wished he had the time to experience what a female felt, but fought the feeling back. Her body returned to an impotent state and he once again took control.

In order to get the medallion, I have to drop the rifle and grab it at about the same time, he thought. *If Beliah has a clue to what is happening before I can get the medallion, we're all through.*

"Shoot him, Missy."

Jason could hear Beliah's command and he felt Missy's body tensing in response. Her finger moved for the trigger and then squeezed. He held her at the first tick of the trigger, but just barely. If Jason was going to make his move, he had to make it now.

"Missy!" Beliah bellowed.

Jason reached out with her left hand and quickly grabbed the medallion, yanking down on the gold chain, snapping it. The medallion fell away and Jason tossed it over Beliah's shoulder, out of immediate reach. Jason and his body fell to the ground as if dead.

50

Tamara watched the scene unfold and disappeared as soon as the field was gone. She knew what had happened to Jason as soon as she saw Missy and his body fall to the ground. He had gotten too attached to the events. He had essentially possessed her body and was now trapped within her. Tamara had to get him out before Beliah regained control.

She winked into the physical as quickly as she had winked out of it. She reappeared kneeling at Missy's feet and reached for the rifle. The weapon felt good in her hands and she pointed it at Beliah, pulling back on the trigger. The rifle released thirty rounds within seconds, but it was only when the last round fired that Tamara realized she was shooting at nothing. Beliah had vanished before the first round had fired.

"Damn," she swore, looking through the smoke of spent gunpowder. She saw Wanda pick up and point the rifle Bill had held on her back at him. "You okay?"

"Yeah, I think so," Wanda said. "What happened?"

"I need help over here," Dunn said. He was leaning over Jason's limp body checking his neck for a pulse.

"His body's fine, Sheriff; it's his spirit I'm worried about." Tamara laid Missy's body out fully prone and began CPR on her. "Help me with this, will you?"

Wanda and Dunn reached Tamara at the same time and Dunn took up the chest compressions: they started a five-to-one count. "One and two and I don't understand and breathe," Dunn said.

"His spirit is in Missy," Tamara said

"Breathe."

"If she dies, he dies."

"Breathe."

"Wanda, take over. I've gotta—"

"Breathe."

"—go in and get him."

They changed places and Wanda mimicked Tamara's actions. She had never done CPR before.

"You'll know I found him when his body starts to move."

"What about her?" Wanda asked between breaths.

"She's dead already. When he starts to move, let her go." And with that, Tamara winked out.

51

Tamara observed Wanda and Dunn administering CPR from roughly four feet above them. She knew she had to act quickly in order to retrieve Jason from Missy's dying body. Like any normal death, as the body shuts down the spirit enters a staging area, preparing itself for final departure. The act was totally involuntary and beyond the control of the spirit host. The spirit was held in a state of suspended animation within the body until the last breath was released.

After weighing her options, she merged with Missy's body. In spite of the danger, she knew it was her only choice. Jason would not be able to respond to her call even if he could sense her. She knew he probably didn't even understand what was happening to him. Based on the conditions within the body he might very well think he was dying and allow nature to take its course.

Tamara found herself inside a dying mind. The brain was busy systematically shutting down the bodily functions in a last ditch effort to stay alive. On the outside her death might appear controlled and organized, but on the inside all hell was breaking loose. She experienced partial memories, recreated from Missy's life, whiz through her consciousness. She encountered the first hints of awareness that signaled Missy's birth. The image didn't disappear after viewing, but remained as an active force in her dying body.

Tamara felt pain and anguish coming, not from without, but from within. The pain was from the past and it was associated with Missy's conception. She was shocked to discover that Missy was the product of a brutal rape, inflicted on her mother from some man close to her, maybe an uncle. The pain stemmed more from the mistrust than the actual crime.

The vision changed into a humanoid creature representing the pain from that trauma. It possessed incredible size compared to the image Missy had of herself. It had a bald head with no ears and thick veins running up its body, terminating at the eyes. Its face was divided vertically with one eye and half of the mouth smiling gently and the other half twisted into an evil snarl of hate and disgust.

This creature was joined immediately by another one almost as hideous. This one evolved from the memory of a two-year-old Missy sitting quietly in a crib while her mother made love to a man not her father, in the same room. No wonder Beliah was able to invade her so quickly, Tamara thought.

The two creatures started to battle and a third creature much different than the first two appeared. This creature was decidedly serene and feminine in appearance. She resembled Missy but with an apparent strength that Tamara never could have known she had. This third creature developed from a cherished moment in kindergarten. Tamara felt the pride Missy had shown after presenting her mother with a hand-print pressed in clay. Tamara felt the tears that Missy's mother shed over the gift. Missy's memories were fighting a battle that had already been lost.

All through her life tiny memories matured into creatures, some good and some bad. In their respective time frames each waged war on the others. The victors joined others of their kind in a forward progression to the present. The closer Tamara got to the final memories the worse they became. Without seeing the outcomes of the earlier battles she knew that evil would win. It always does in cases like this.

The memories were battling over Jason's spirit, however. He had nothing to do with Missy's life, and now he was a prisoner of a war between the forces of good and evil raging within her. His spirit would be destroyed if Tamara didn't act soon. Frantically, she called out to him, searching the latest memories for him. [Jason. Can you hear me?] The words became memories themselves and spread out from her filling the entire mind of Missy. Some of the creatures paused as if curious, but then continued their struggle.

[Jason!]

[Jason? My name is Missy.]

It felt like Jason and Tamara continued to inspect each fresh memory for his essence; he would be found there. [Jason, you're not Missy. These memories don't belong to you. Come to me now before you're destroyed. It's Tamara, come to me.]

[Tamara? Why are you here? Am I dying?]

[Jason, Missy's dying and you are trapped within her. Remember the field and Wanda?] She hoped his memories of recent events would shatter his faith in the memories that now defined the life of Missy.

[Yeah, I... Tamara?]

[Yes, it's me. You've got to get out. You've been trapped within her. Search me out and I will show you the way back. Hurry, Jason. There's not much time.]

Tamara felt a tug on her spirit coming from deep within Missy's mind. It felt like Jason and she spooled herself out to him in a long, thin, silvery cord. She felt him lock on to her cord and he began to snake his way through it. The slow trickle that was Jason began to merge with her. The flow increased and she became filled with his warmth. Like him, she enjoyed the intimate connection and delighted in their union.

[Tamara, I'm still not sure what happened. Can—]

[Follow me!] And with that, the two of them departed from Missy's body, it expiring a moment later.

52

Tamara materialized in a prone position along side Jason. They were wrapped tightly in each others' embrace. Relaxing her hold without letting go, she looked up and discovered Wanda and Dunn staring down at them with puzzled looks on their faces.

"I can't get use to this," Dunn said. "One minute I see Jason start to move and I rush over here to check his pulse. The next minute you're knocking me over with your arms locked around him."

"It's like, blink, you're here," Wanda said, helping Tamara to her feet.

"What a ride!" Jason said, obviously very happy to be back in his own body. He sat up and pulled his knees to his chest.

"You okay, kid?" Dunn asked.

"Yeah." Then reaching up for Tamara's hand he said, "You could've been trapped in there just like me, huh?"

Tamara pulled him up and said, "As long as we made it."

"It's true, isn't it? We both could have been trapped."

Tamara shrugged.

Jason looked at her, and in that moment he knew he loved her. Not just a teenage crush, but genuine love. She had risked herself to save him. The moment passed. "What happened to Beliah?" he asked.

"He just disappeared," Wanda said. "Poof!"

"It's not over yet, buddy. We have to go after him."

Jason smiled at Tamara. That was the first time she ever called him that. It sounded good coming from her. "So how do we find him?"

"There's only one place he could have gone. He went ethereal and is biding his time until we find him."

"So what are we waiting for? Let's get him."

"Not so fast, Jason. That's his element. He wants us to follow him there. Chances are he'll be alone. Even so, we're no match for him."

"Then what do we do?"

"We outsmart him. I think you threw him off. I don't think he planned for you being here. Wanda... probably, but you, you're different, Jason. You're an unknown variable."

"Yeah, what about me?" Wanda looked impatient. "You told me I was like you and Jason, but all I seem to be is in the way."

"Wanda, if we had more time I could guide you through the spirit world and show you how to become."

"Why didn't Beliah come after us while we were in Missy's body?" Jason asked, returning the subject to Beliah.

"He was hoping Missy's body would die before we could get out. Once we were in her, there wasn't much he could do to us, short of destroying her body, and that would have released us anyway. No, he hoped the death of the body would take care of us."

"Can he hear us?" Dunn asked.

"I don't think so," Jason answered. "I can never hear when I am out of body."

"You're right, but he can see us," Tamara said. "He's probably watching us right now."

Goose bumps ran up Jason's arms. "So what do we do?" He asked again.

"Wanda, you're coming with us. If he didn't figure on Jason, he might just believe that you're a Traveler, too. We'll use that to confuse him."

"We can't beat him, can we Tamara?" Jason looked doubtful.

"No. But we can run him off. It's been done before. Your town's not lost yet, Sheriff."

"What do you want me to do?" he asked.

"There's gonna be a lot of sleepy people calling you soon. Beliah put all but his people in a deep sleep. They should be waking soon with a lot of questions. I'll leave it up to you to decide what to tell them."

"Uhh, thanks," Dunn said, his thoughts whirling, making him dizzy.

"Oh," Wanda said. "After everyone disappeared, I picked this up. He left it." She produced the medallion from her back pocket and held it up to Tamara.

"That's great. Our odds just got better. Jason, put that around your neck and grab Wanda's hand."

He did, but the medallion had changed now. It didn't seem as powerful and frightening as before. It also didn't feel as heavy as he thought it might. He took hold of Wanda's hand and Tamara took the other. She slipped her hand in his and completed the circle. Tamara's gentle, reassuring squeeze gave him comfort. A moment later, Jason found himself in that other reality. The three of them were still joined, but they lacked any real shape. Judging by the other two he discovered they were gaseous, florescent balloons tied to each other by three shimmering cords.

They were horizontal and triangular in shape with each of them forming one point. The medallion, now as large as they, filled the center of the triangle. It was perpendicular to them and rotated irregularly, with the front of the medallion picking up speed whenever it faced in his or Tamara's direction and slowing when it faced Wanda.

[Tam—]

She cut him off. There would be no talking.

They changed orientation at Tamara's lead and positioned their triangular shape vertically with Wanda at the top and Tamara and himself forming the base. Much to his surprise, the medallion didn't move with them. It remained stationary and now he viewed it on edge. The medallion spun in a clockwise direction, the face pointed either forward or backward depending on the spin.

In this configuration it rotated at a constant speed, with the energy coming from him and Tamara and flowing into Wanda. He understood completely what Tamara was trying to accomplish. The medallion acted like a gigantic capacitor, storing their energy and redistributing it through Wanda.

Jason felt the field forming around them even before he could perceive it. The feeling was an unmistakable bleeding of his energy. But the drop in power was compensated by the intensity of the field. The field's color was sky blue in direct contrast to the chalky, almost powdery, texture of this reality. He narrowed and intensified his focus and felt the vibrations of sound. It was more of a pulsation than anything audible and a clear sound-picture formed in his mind. It resembled the echo of a Chinese gong. It was coming from them. Together, they were making beautiful music.

Tamara spoke at last. [I've created an energy cell. As long as we remain within it, Beliah can't manipulate us.]

[What do you mean by that?] Jason asked.

Tamara sighed. [I can't lie to you. This is his element. If we give him the chance, he will turn us against one another. He could make us see and feel whatever he wants. This cell is our only sanctuary.]

Tamara couldn't lie to them even if she wanted to and Jason knew it. While in this state, nothing could be hidden from him. However, it wasn't what she said that bothered him, it was how she felt. Tamara was scared.

[Will this hold?]

[I don't know.]

Jason was caught off guard when their field powered up. As if in response, a sphere of ebony formed in this reality, almost a hole swallowing everything around it. There was no mistaking it, that blackness was Beliah. His appearance drained all excess energy, forcing itself on their field. The energy transfer left Jason tired and crippled. The field flickered a moment and then intensified again. He watched as new energy flowed out of them and into the medallion. The crystal center emitted a beam of indigo and the field was made whole once again.

[I see you have something that belongs to me, Tamara.] Beliah said.

Tamara didn't respond. Instead, Jason felt the field intensify and swell into an explosive orb. Just when he thought it had reached critical overload, the crystal emitted another beam, only this one was directed at Beliah.

The black pit in space that was Beliah swallowed the beam without any noticeable change in his appearance save one: His size decreased slightly. The smaller Beliah seemed darker and yet his omnipotence softened slightly. It only lasted for an instant and then he expanded to four times as large as before, the edges of his sphere fading to white instead of creating a solid, well defined border. With the increase in size came another power drain to their field, only this time it was Tamara's side that weakened. She had taken on the full burden of the drain.

[Tamara, are you okay?] Jason asked.

[That was very foolish, Tamara,] Beliah said. [If you die, who will train your apprentices? Shall I have the honor? Come Tamara, you can't beat me. Join me and together we can rule the world of the mortals. You will govern and I will—]

[You'll set yourself up as a god. Never! I will never allow it, Proteus. I will fight you to the end of the age.]

[You use my ancient name. I'm surprised you remembered it. How kind of you to dig up a past that no longer exist.] A blast of midnight came at them without warning, encasing them in a pocket of dark electricity that slowly ate its way into their field.

[It's not gonna hold,] Tamara howled.

Jason felt the field weaken all around them. He knew without Tamara having to say it that without Wanda they might be able to repel the attack. The smaller field would possess the same amount of energy and thus be stronger. Wanda was nothing more than a receptacle of the reserved energy and a useless drain on the shield.

Wanda must have known it too, for she said, [Let me go. There's no sense in all of us dying.]

[Forget it,] Tamara said. [If we can't hold him now, then he'll just get us one at a time.] Tamara paused for just a second and then said, [But maybe that's what we should do. Jason, break free and take Wanda with you.]

[But—]

[No time for questions. Do it.] That last was an order. This was no time for a discussion.

Tamara was right. Jason could see globs of the black electricity seeping through the field. If she had an idea he would have to trust that it would work. He retracted the silver cord connecting him to her and reached out to Wanda with it. She did the same and the two cords became one. Their appearance looked like that of a dumbbell, two small orbs of energy connected together by a delicate, silver cord. They began to spin around each other, gradually moving away from Tamara and the medallion. The field separated and part of it went with them and the remainder stayed with Tamara.

The flowing blackness trailed off them and attacked Tamara with unbelievable speed, enveloping her completely. The blue of her field vanished within the dark and Jason lost all contact with her. The warmth he always felt in her presence was gone. It was replaced by freezing cold. *The grave must feel like this*, he thought. Beliah expanded in size again, now consuming all of space, blocking out the white reality in ever increasing shades of gray. The expansion lightened his color, changing it from black to charcoal with a spot of blue in the center. That spot was Tamara.

[Now it's your turn.] Beliah said, transferring his thoughts towards them.

Their field of blue was the only existence beyond the gray, and that was being assaulted even now.

[Jason, what are we gonna do?]

[I don't know.]

[I'll tell you what to do. Prepare to die, fools. You are mine.]

53

Jason was at a loss for what to do. He assumed Tamara had a plan, but from the looks of things she was in as much trouble as they were, if not more. He studied the small, faded blue dot in the center of that swirling gray mass, searching for some sign that she had everything under control. The dot didn't change size, shape or color. It just sat in all of that gray.

All of that gray?

His next move flashed across his mind faster than his ability to fully understand the implications. He merged with Wanda, just like he had done with Tamara before. The union with her was just as intimate but less passionate than with Tamara. They were now a single, gaseous ball of blue light, rapidly moving closer toward Tamara. *This has gotta work*, he thought. *Why else would she have separated us?*

Either knowing what they were about to do or simply closing in for the kill, Beliah contracted in size, retracing the same path in as he earlier followed out, the shades of black increasing as he got smaller. The gray had been an illusion. Jason thought of Beliah as two-dimensional and expected Tamara to occupy his surface like a coin on a round table. Instead, she was within him. And now, so was he.

Jason found himself traveling through a dark, shadowy tunnel devoid of light. Tamara was still the most vibrant object in sight, but Beliah was shrinking fast. Soon, Jason wouldn't be able to tell them apart. He had to reach her before Beliah coalesced completely for his plan to work.

[Tamara!] He didn't know if she could hear him or not, but he needed to try.

As if in response to his call, tiny fractures appeared in the dot that was Tamara and sprinkled the dark, gloomy tunnel with a bluish white light. The fractures multiplied and Jason took that as his sign to act. Removing as much stored energy from Wanda as he dared, Jason directed a narrow shaft of energy into one of the fractures. He felt himself bleeding away as Tamara drew more of the energy out of him. Her color was growing brighter and Jason could see the medallion glowing fiercely inside of her.

[NO!] Beliah screamed.

I must be doing something right, Jason thought as the last bit of energy flowed out of him. *Tamara is using our consciousness as a weapon. At least I will die with her. I'm sorry, Wanda.* He knew she didn't hear him and he didn't have the energy to communicate with her. Their time was up and his only regret was that he wouldn't live long enough to become a Traveler like Tamara. *I love you Tamara.*

53

The blast hurled Jason from the ethereal reality back into the physical/material. He didn't have a clue as to what had happened and it was only his throbbing head that reminded him that in the material world he felt pain. He was on his back and felt a stabbing pain in his shoulder. He rolled off his shoulder and the pain went away only to return once he rolled back. *I'm lying on a rock*, he thought. He moved one shaky hand in an effort to remove it, but failed and didn't have the strength for a second try.

"Jason? Are you okay?"

"Yeah Sheriff," he said weakly. "But don't ask me to tell you what happened. How's Wanda?"

"She looks as bad as you, kid. The two of you could be bookends for The History of War series."

Jason tried to laugh but only managed a smile. "Is Tamara here?"

"I don't think she made it. I mean, the three of you left, then I felt something like a strong wind, and then you and Wanda twitched—well, your bodies at least—and then you woke up. That's all I saw. You were only gone a second, if that. Is she still there?"

"I don't think so."

"What about Beliah?"

Jason was feeling stronger even though his head still pounded. He sat up on one elbow and glanced at Wanda. She was moving her arms around sluggishly, reaching for her head. "It's still there, Wanda. Your head I mean."

She rolled her head towards Jason and smiled. "Thanks," she whispered.

"He's gone, Sheriff," Jason said.

"Dead?"

"No." Jason didn't know how he knew that, but he did.

"Will he be back?"

"No—at least not anytime soon."

"I'm sorry," Dunn said. "I didn't know her as well as you did, but I could tell she was a good woman."

Jason's eyes stung with tears and he allowed them to come. Sitting up he put his head between his knees and silently wept for those he had lost. He cried for Tommy; he cried for Tonka; he cried for all the people that died because of Beliah. But especially he cried for Tamara.

"You should be happy you're alive, buddy."

Jason jumped to his feet out of fright. There, standing before him, was Tamara looking just as beautiful as the night he first dreamed of her. "Tamara!"

"What did you think? That I would let you take all of the credit?"

"You're alive!"

"Lighten up, kid. You should know that energy can't be destroyed—"

"Yeah, it just changes forms. But what happened?"

"Beliah did just as I predicted. He didn't want me, he wanted you. Once he thought he had me contained, he went straight for you. I was hoping you would figure out that his size has nothing to do with his power."

"I did. When I saw him turning gray, I figured he was stretching himself too thin and wouldn't be able to consolidate his power in time to stop our combined attack."

"Whoa," Wanda said sitting up and holding her head in her hands. "Slow down. I was there and I still don't know what happened."

Jason spoke excitedly. "Don't you see? When we separated, Beliah—"

"Got cocky," Tamara said. Then growing serious, "He thought he could overwhelm you with his size. If it wasn't for the reflective power of the medallion, he would have had us. We got lucky."

Dunn asked, "So where's he now?'

"He's gone. He was hurt by the battle and will go into hiding for a while to heal. He'll probably go to his home world. Hell, we blasted him all over known reality. I'm sure it will take several cycles of this time-frame before he tries again. He needs to consolidate his power again. I don't think he will be back any time soon."

"What about you, Tamara. What's next?" It was the question Jason dreaded to ask, but he needed to know.

She smiled at him, lovingly. She knew his thoughts. After all, they had joined together in the most intimate way known in existence. "I must pursue him wherever he may go. It is my purpose."

"I understand," he said despondently. "Will I ever see you again?"

"Jason, I couldn't leave without you. You're my love. Don't you know that?"

"You want me to go with you?"

She put one finger lightly under his chin and pulled him to her. Her full lips parted and she affectionately touched her lips to his. The warmth of their kiss brought him closer and they embraced passionately. "Of course," she whispered.

Wanda asked, "You want to get a room or something?" They all laughed at that causing Jason to pull away, head down, slightly embarrassed.

"But Jason," Tamara said, "You'll have to die. You'll have to give up your body. It's the only way."

"My parents—"

"Will be told that you died like the others," Dunn said. "I'll tell them that Beliah killed you like all the others."

"You're outside the restraints of time, now." Tamara said. "Your physical body will be too much of a drain on your travels. You have to leave it behind. Do you think you can do it, my love?"

"Not a problem, as long as I am with you." It was strange, Jason thought. He still loved his parents, but he didn't feel any familiarity with them now. It was like he had outgrown them, like a boyhood puppy that had grown old. He could leave them. They were only mere reflections in a prism of light: An illusion.

Wanda asked, "What about me? Am I going too?"

"No, not now. You still have much to learn and you aren't prepared to live out eternity where we are going. When it's time, we'll be back for you. Sheriff, I don't envy you. What are you going to tell them?"

"I'll think of something," he said. "But, if you're goin', go. It's gonna be hard enough without you disappearing after the fact."

"Yes. Jason, if you're ready we can leave."

"I'm ready."

"If you want you can bring Tonka."

"He's dead, Tamara."

"As long as you have an imagination, nothing need ever die."

"You mean recreate him like you do with your body or car."

"Yes."

"Nah. He wouldn't be the same. Maybe I'll meet another dog somewhere."

"There are entities out there that express themselves just like a loyal dog would. Their energy never disappears, it just changes form." They smiled at each other and the smile told Tamara that Jason was ready. "Then we go."

"Yeah, we go."

And with that, Tamara and Jason winked out.

The End